The Mermaid's Whisper

Fairy tales, Folk tales, Legends & Mythology, Volume 2

Patrick William Lee

Published by Patrick William Lee, 2024.

Table of Contents

To the dreamers who find magic in the whispers of the sea,

To those who believe in the power of friendship and the strength of
the human spirit,

And to my family, for their unwavering support and endless
inspiration.

May the tides of adventure always lead you to wonder and discovery.

Chapter 1: The Enchanted Shore

Introduction to the Coastal Village of Marinia

Nestled along the rugged coastline, the village of Marinia was a place where the sea sang its eternal lullaby, where waves whispered secrets to the shore, and where the air was always tinged with the scent of salt and adventure. Marinia, with its quaint cottages and cobblestone streets, seemed timeless, untouched by the rush of the world beyond the horizon. Here, life moved to the rhythm of the tides, and the villagers lived in harmony with the ocean that provided their sustenance and shaped their traditions.

The people of Marinia were a hardy folk, bound together by their shared love and respect for the sea. Generations of fishermen, sailors, and seafarers called this village home, passing down stories of the ocean's mysteries from one generation to the next. Among these tales, none were more cherished than the legends of the mermaids. It was said that the mermaids were guardians of the sea, protectors of its treasures, and that they sometimes ventured close to shore to guide lost sailors or to bestow blessings upon those they deemed worthy.

These stories were woven into the fabric of Marinia's culture, celebrated in songs and festivals, and depicted in the intricate carvings that adorned the village's buildings and boats. Every child in Marinia grew up hearing the tales of these mystical beings, and every adult carried the lore in their hearts, a comforting reminder of the enchantment that lay just beyond the waves.

Meet the Protagonist, Elara

AMONG THE VILLAGERS was a young girl named Elara, whose heart beat with an unquenchable curiosity about the sea. Elara was the daughter of a fisherman, a man named Finn, who was as rugged and dependable as the boats he sailed. Her mother, Aisling, had passed away when Elara was just a child, leaving her with faint memories of a soft voice singing lullabies and the scent of lavender that always lingered around her mother.

Elara had inherited her mother's spirit of wonder and her father's resilience. With long, chestnut hair that caught the sun's light and eyes as blue as the deepest part of the ocean, she was a striking figure, often seen wandering the shoreline with her gaze fixed on the horizon. Elara's bond with the sea was evident to all who knew her. She would spend hours collecting shells, watching the waves, and dreaming of the underwater world that the mermaid stories spoke of.

Finn, though deeply protective of his only child, understood her fascination. He would often tell her tales of his own encounters with the sea's mysteries, embellishing them with a twinkle in his eye that suggested he believed in the magic as much as she did. It was from him that Elara learned to read the tides, to navigate by the stars, and to fish with the skill and patience of a seasoned sailor.

Despite her father's teachings and the village's embrace, Elara often felt a restlessness, a yearning for something more. She longed for an adventure that would take her beyond the familiar shores of Marinia, into the depths of the sea where the mermaids dwelled. This desire was both a blessing and a curse, for it made her feel alive but also made her aware of the boundaries that confined her.

Elara Finds an Ancient Shell

IT WAS ON A CRISP MORNING in early spring, as the first light of dawn painted the sky in hues of pink and gold, that Elara set out on one of her solitary walks along the beach. The tide was low, revealing a stretch of sand scattered with driftwood, seaweed, and shells of all shapes and sizes. Elara loved these moments, when the world was quiet and the air was fresh, filled with the promise of discovery.

As she strolled, her eyes scanning the ground for any new treasures, something unusual caught her attention. Partially buried in the sand, glinting in the soft light, was a shell unlike any she had ever seen. It was large, almost the size of her hand, with a spiral shape that twisted elegantly inward. The shell's surface was smooth and iridescent, reflecting the colors of the sky and sea. But what truly captivated Elara were the strange engravings that adorned it, intricate patterns that seemed to pulse with a life of their own.

Kneeling down, Elara gently unearthed the shell, her fingers tracing the delicate lines of the carvings. She felt a sudden rush of warmth, a tingling sensation that traveled up her arm and filled her with a sense of wonder and anticipation. This was no ordinary shell; it felt ancient and powerful, as if it held within it the secrets of the ocean.

Elara's heart pounded with excitement. She knew she had found something extraordinary, something that might hold the key to the mysteries she had always yearned to uncover. Clutching the shell to her chest, she made her way back to the village, eager to show her father and to seek the wisdom of the village elder, a woman named Maelis who was known for her knowledge of the old ways and the ancient legends.

The Village Elder's Insight

MAELIS LIVED IN A SMALL cottage at the edge of the village, surrounded by a garden filled with herbs and flowers. The villagers often came to her for remedies and advice, trusting in her deep connection to the natural world. Elara had always admired Maelis, finding comfort in her gentle demeanor and the wealth of stories she carried.

Arriving at Maelis's door, Elara knocked softly, her excitement barely contained. The elder opened the door, her eyes bright with curiosity as she saw the young girl standing there, holding the unusual shell.

"Elara, my dear, what brings you here so early?" Maelis asked, her voice warm and inviting.

"I found something on the shore," Elara replied, holding out the shell for Maelis to see. "It's unlike any shell I've ever seen. I thought you might know what it is."

Maelis took the shell from Elara's hands, her eyes widening as she examined the engravings. She ran her fingers over the patterns, her expression growing thoughtful. After a few moments, she looked up at Elara, her gaze filled with a mixture of awe and concern.

"This is indeed a rare find, Elara," Maelis said softly. "These engravings are ancient symbols, linked to the old legends of the sea. It is said that such shells are used by the merfolk to communicate with the human world. They are imbued with powerful magic."

Elara's heart leaped at Maelis's words. "Does that mean this shell could help me find a mermaid?" she asked eagerly.

Maelis smiled, her eyes twinkling. "Perhaps. But you must be cautious, Elara. The sea is full of wonders, but also dangers. If this shell has found its way to you, it is for a reason. You must be prepared for whatever journey lies ahead."

Elara nodded, her determination unwavering. She felt a deep connection to the shell, as if it were calling her to fulfill a destiny she had always known was hers. With Maelis's guidance and her own unyielding spirit, she was ready to face whatever challenges the sea might present.

The Whisper of Destiny

THAT NIGHT, AS ELARA lay in her bed, the shell placed carefully on her bedside table, she felt a sense of anticipation thrumming through her veins. She could hardly sleep, her mind racing with thoughts of what the shell might reveal and what adventures awaited her.

In the quiet of the night, just as she was beginning to drift off, Elara heard a faint whisper. It was a soft, melodic voice, unlike anything she had ever heard before. The voice seemed to be coming from the shell, its tone both soothing and urgent.

"Elara," the voice whispered, "you have found the Shell of Seraphina. I am Seraphina, a mermaid bound by a curse. I need your help to break free. Come to the hidden cove at dawn, and I will explain everything."

Elara sat up, her heart pounding with excitement and a hint of fear. This was the moment she had been waiting for, the beginning of the adventure she had always dreamed of. She knew she had to answer the call.

As the first light of dawn began to creep over the horizon, Elara rose from her bed, dressed quickly, and grabbed the shell. She slipped out of her house, the village still shrouded in the peaceful silence of early morning, and made her way to the shore.

The Hidden Cove

FOLLOWING THE WHISPERS of the shell, Elara walked along the beach, her eyes scanning the rocky cliffs that lined the shore. She had explored these cliffs many times, but today, guided by the shell's magic, she noticed a narrow path that led to a secluded cove hidden from view.

With a deep breath, Elara stepped onto the path, feeling a sense of destiny guiding her every step. The path wound through the cliffs, eventually opening up to a small, sheltered cove where the water was calm and clear, reflecting the golden light of the rising sun.

In the center of the cove, just beneath the surface of the water, Elara saw a figure shimmering in the morning light. It was a mermaid, her long hair flowing like liquid silver, her tail a dazzling array of colors that sparkled in the sunlight. She was beautiful and ethereal, exactly as Elara had always imagined.

"Elara," the mermaid's voice called softly, the same voice she had heard from the shell. "I am Seraphina. Thank you for coming."

Elara stepped closer to the water's edge, her heart racing with a mixture of awe and excitement. "Seraphina," she said, her voice trembling slightly. "I've always dreamed of meeting a mermaid. How can I help you?"

Seraphina smiled, her eyes filled with gratitude and hope. "I have been trapped here by a curse placed upon me by the sea witch Morgana. I can only communicate through this enchanted shell. You, Elara, are the one who can break the curse and set me free. But it will not be easy. You must embark on a quest to gather the ingredients for a potion that will break the spell. Will you help me?"

Elara felt a surge of determination. This was the adventure she had been waiting for, a chance to prove her courage and to fulfill her dreams. "Yes, Seraphina," she said firmly. "I will help you break the curse. Tell me what I need to do."

The Beginning of the Quest

SERAPHINA'S EYES SPARKLED with relief and determination. "Thank you, Elara. The ingredients you need to find are rare and guarded by powerful forces. The first is the Moonflower petals, which can only be found in the Whispering Woods. The second is the Echoing Crystals from the Mountain of Echoes. The third is the Golden Seaweed from the Sunken Ruins, and the fourth is the Shadow Berries from the Island of Shadows."

Elara listened intently, memorizing each location and its corresponding ingredient. She knew the journey ahead would be fraught with challenges, but she felt ready to face them.

"Take this shell with you," Seraphina continued. "It will guide you and allow us to stay in contact. Remember, Elara, the sea is watching over you. Trust in your heart and your courage."

With Seraphina's words echoing in her mind, Elara nodded, her resolve firm. She slipped the shell into her bag and turned to leave the cove, ready to begin her quest.

As she made her way back to the village, the first rays of sunlight casting a golden glow over the landscape, Elara felt a sense of purpose and excitement. She was no longer just a curious girl dreaming of the sea; she was on a mission to break a curse and to uncover the mysteries of the ocean.

The journey ahead would test her in ways she could not yet imagine, but Elara knew that she was ready. With the support of her father, the wisdom of Maelis, and the guidance of Seraphina, she would face whatever challenges lay ahead and emerge stronger and wiser.

And so, with the village of Marinia waking up to another day, Elara set off on her grand adventure, her heart filled with hope and her spirit unyielding. The sea, with all its magic and mystery, awaited her, and she was ready to embrace her destiny.

Chapter 2: The Mysterious Voice

The Whisper from the Shell

Elara returned to her room, her heart still racing from her morning encounter with the mermaid Seraphina. The shell, now resting on her bedside table, seemed to pulse with an inner light, casting faint, shimmering patterns on the walls. She couldn't shake the feeling that her life had irrevocably changed. That night, sleep eluded her as she lay in bed, staring at the shell and contemplating the journey that lay ahead.

As the village of Marinia slumbered under a canopy of stars, Elara found herself drawn to the shell. She reached out and touched it, feeling a warmth emanate from its smooth surface. Almost immediately, she heard the soft, melodic whisper of Seraphina's voice.

"Elara," the voice began, filling the room with a sense of calm and wonder, "there is much I need to tell you. Please, come to the hidden cove at dawn."

Elara sat up, her mind racing with questions. She had so much to ask, so much she wanted to know about the mermaid and the curse that bound her. But the shell offered no more answers that night, its whisper fading into silence. Determined to learn more, Elara resolved to visit the cove as soon as the first light of day broke over the horizon.

The Journey to the Hidden Cove

THE FOLLOWING MORNING, Elara rose before the sun, her excitement tempered by a sense of purpose. She dressed quickly, slipping the enchanted shell into her satchel before heading out. The village was still shrouded in the tranquil hush of pre-dawn, the only sounds the gentle lapping of waves and the occasional cry of a seabird.

Elara made her way along the familiar path to the shore, her feet moving swiftly over the sandy beach. The sky was just beginning to lighten, a faint glow heralding the arrival of a new day. Guided by an inexplicable sense of direction,

Elara followed the coastline, her eyes scanning the rocky cliffs for any sign of the hidden path she had discovered the previous day.

As she approached the spot where the path should have been, Elara felt a gentle tug, almost as if the shell were guiding her. She paused, looking more closely at the rocks, and there it was—a narrow, winding trail that led through the cliffs and down to the secluded cove.

Taking a deep breath, Elara stepped onto the path, her heart pounding with anticipation. The trail was steep and uneven, but she navigated it with ease, her excitement propelling her forward. Finally, she emerged into the hidden cove, a small, sheltered bay where the water was calm and clear, reflecting the soft hues of dawn.

Meeting Seraphina

AS ELARA APPROACHED the water's edge, she saw the familiar figure of Seraphina just beneath the surface. The mermaid's long, silver hair floated around her like a halo, and her tail shimmered with iridescent colors. Seraphina's eyes, a deep, otherworldly blue, locked onto Elara's, filled with a mixture of hope and gratitude.

"Thank you for coming, Elara," Seraphina said, her voice carrying a musical quality that seemed to harmonize with the sounds of the sea. "I know you must have many questions. I will do my best to answer them."

Elara knelt at the water's edge, her curiosity overcoming her initial awe. "Seraphina, how did you end up here? And what can I do to help you?"

Seraphina sighed, her expression turning somber. "I was once the guardian of this part of the sea, entrusted with protecting its creatures and maintaining its balance. But my role drew the ire of Morgana, a powerful sea witch who sought to control these waters for her own gain. When I refused to yield to her demands, she cursed me, binding me to this cove and stripping me of my ability to communicate freely."

Elara listened intently, her heart aching for the mermaid's plight. "That's terrible," she said softly. "How can we break the curse?"

The Curse and the Quest

SERAPHINA'S GAZE GREW more intense. "The curse is powerful, woven with dark magic. To break it, we must create a potion using four rare ingredients: Moonflower petals, Echoing Crystals, Golden Seaweed, and Shadow Berries. These ingredients are scattered across the land and sea, each guarded by formidable challenges."

Elara nodded, determination hardening her resolve. "I'm ready to face whatever comes. Where should I begin?"

Seraphina smiled, a glimmer of hope lighting her eyes. "The first ingredient is the Moonflower petals, found only in the Whispering Woods. The woods are a place of mystery, where the trees seem to whisper secrets to those who listen. You will need to be cautious and brave."

Elara felt a thrill of anticipation. "I'll leave for the Whispering Woods at once," she said. "But how will I know where to find the Moonflowers?"

Seraphina held out her hand, and Elara saw a small, glowing crystal nestled in her palm. "Take this," Seraphina said. "It is a guiding stone. It will glow brighter as you get closer to the Moonflowers. Trust in its light, and it will lead you to what you seek."

Elara accepted the crystal, feeling its warmth against her skin. "Thank you, Seraphina. I promise I won't let you down."

The mermaid's smile broadened, her eyes shining with gratitude. "I know you won't, Elara. You have a brave heart and a noble spirit. The sea chose you for this task, and I believe in you."

With those words, Elara felt a surge of confidence. She tucked the guiding stone into her satchel alongside the shell and stood, ready to begin her journey. "I'll return as soon as I have the Moonflower petals," she promised.

As Elara turned to leave the cove, Seraphina's voice followed her, a soft whisper that seemed to blend with the sound of the waves. "Be safe, Elara. And remember, you are not alone. The sea is with you."

The Whispering Woods

ELARA MADE HER WAY back to the village, her mind focused on the task ahead. She gathered a few supplies for her journey, including food, water, and a sturdy walking stick. She also told her father, Finn, about her plans, carefully omitting the more fantastical details. Finn, ever supportive of his daughter's adventurous spirit, wished her luck and reminded her to be careful.

The Whispering Woods lay to the north of Marinia, a dense forest known for its tall, ancient trees and the eerie whispers that filled the air. The villagers spoke of the woods with a mixture of reverence and caution, for while they were a place of beauty and wonder, they also held secrets and dangers.

As Elara approached the edge of the forest, she felt a shiver of excitement and trepidation. The trees towered above her, their branches forming a thick canopy that filtered the sunlight into a soft, green glow. She could hear the faint whisper of leaves rustling in the breeze, a sound that seemed almost like voices murmuring just beyond her hearing.

Taking a deep breath, Elara stepped into the woods, feeling the cool, mossy ground beneath her feet. She reached into her satchel and pulled out the guiding stone, holding it in her palm. The stone glowed with a soft, ethereal light, pulsing gently as if in tune with her heartbeat.

Elara followed the stone's light, moving deeper into the forest. The trees seemed to close in around her, their whispers growing louder and more distinct. She could almost make out words, but they remained just beyond her understanding, like a song sung in a language she didn't know.

As she walked, Elara felt a growing sense of unease. The forest was beautiful, but it was also unsettling, as if it were watching her, judging her worthiness. She reminded herself of Seraphina's words and the importance of her quest, using her determination to push through her fear.

The Guardians of the Moonflowers

AFTER HOURS OF WALKING, the guiding stone's light grew brighter, signaling that she was getting closer to the Moonflowers. Elara's spirits lifted, and she quickened her pace, eager to complete the first part of her journey.

Eventually, she came upon a small clearing bathed in a soft, silver light. In the center of the clearing grew a cluster of Moonflowers, their petals glowing with a pale, otherworldly luminescence. Elara approached the flowers with reverence, marveling at their delicate beauty.

Just as she was about to pick the first petal, a voice rang out, clear and commanding. "Who dares to disturb the Moonflowers?"

Elara froze, her heart pounding. She turned to see a figure step out from the shadows of the trees. It was a woman, tall and regal, with hair that flowed like silver and eyes that shone with an inner light. She wore a gown made of leaves and flowers, and her presence seemed to command the very forest around her.

"I am Elara," she said, her voice steady despite her fear. "I seek the Moonflower petals to break a curse and free a mermaid named Seraphina."

The woman studied her for a moment, her expression unreadable. "I am Lyria, the guardian of the Whispering Woods," she said finally. "These flowers are under my protection. What makes you think you are worthy of taking them?"

Elara took a deep breath, summoning her courage. "I am on a quest to gather the ingredients for a potion to break Seraphina's curse. She has been bound by a sea witch's dark magic, and only these petals can help free her. I am willing to face any challenge to prove my worth."

Lyria's eyes softened, and she nodded slowly. "Very well, Elara. The Moonflowers are indeed powerful, and their protection is not given lightly. You must prove your worthiness by passing a test of courage and purity of heart."

Elara nodded, her resolve firm. "I am ready."

Lyria raised her hands, and the clearing began to shimmer with magic. "Your test is this: You must navigate the Maze of Reflections. It is a place where your deepest fears and insecurities will be laid bare. Only by facing and overcoming them can you prove your worth."

With those words, the ground beneath Elara's feet shifted, and she found herself standing at the entrance of a labyrinth made of shimmering mirrors. The walls of the maze reflected her image back at her from every angle, creating a dizzying effect.

Taking a deep breath, Elara stepped into the maze, her heart pounding with a mixture of fear and determination. She knew that this test would not be easy, but she also knew that she could not fail. Seraphina was counting on her.

The Maze of Reflections

AS ELARA WALKED DEEPER into the maze, she felt a growing sense of unease. The mirrors reflected not just her physical appearance, but also her thoughts and emotions. She saw herself as a child, grieving the loss of her mother. She saw the moments of doubt and insecurity that had plagued her over the years. Each reflection seemed to taunt her, highlighting her fears and weaknesses.

Elara forced herself to keep moving, refusing to be paralyzed by her own reflections. She reminded herself of the strength and courage that had brought her this far. She had faced loss and hardship before, and she would not be defeated by her own mind.

As she navigated the maze, Elara encountered reflections that seemed to speak to her, their voices echoing in her mind.

"You're not strong enough," one reflection whispered.

"You'll never succeed," another taunted.

Elara clenched her fists, fighting back the tears that threatened to spill over. "I am strong enough," she said aloud, her voice echoing in the maze. "I will succeed."

With each step, she felt her resolve strengthen. She began to focus on the positive reflections, the moments of courage and determination that had defined her. She saw herself standing up to bullies as a child, comforting her father during difficult times, and embarking on this quest with unwavering determination.

Slowly but surely, the negative reflections began to fade, replaced by images of strength and resilience. Elara felt a sense of clarity and peace wash over her, as if a weight had been lifted from her shoulders.

Finally, she reached the center of the maze, where a single, clear mirror stood. In its reflection, she saw herself as she truly was—strong, brave, and determined. She smiled, feeling a surge of pride and confidence.

"You have passed the test," Lyria's voice echoed through the maze. "You have proven your courage and purity of heart."

The maze dissolved around her, and Elara found herself back in the clearing, standing before Lyria. The guardian smiled warmly and handed her a small pouch filled with Moonflower petals.

"You have earned these, Elara," Lyria said. "May they help you in your quest to free Seraphina."

Elara accepted the pouch with gratitude, her heart swelling with pride. "Thank you, Lyria. I will not forget your kindness."

Returning to Seraphina

WITH THE MOONFLOWER petals in hand, Elara made her way back to the hidden cove. The journey through the Whispering Woods had been challenging, but it had also strengthened her resolve and deepened her understanding of her own strength.

As she approached the cove, she saw Seraphina waiting for her, a look of hopeful anticipation in her eyes. Elara knelt at the water's edge and held out the pouch of Moonflower petals.

"I have the petals, Seraphina," she said, her voice filled with pride. "What do we do next?"

Seraphina's eyes sparkled with gratitude and relief. "Thank you, Elara. The first ingredient is ours. Now we must gather the Echoing Crystals from the Mountain of Echoes. It will be a difficult journey, but I have faith in you."

Elara nodded, feeling a renewed sense of determination. "I will head to the mountain at once. We will break this curse, Seraphina. I promise."

Seraphina smiled, her eyes shining with hope. "I know you will, Elara. You are a true friend and a brave soul. The sea is with you, always."

With those words, Elara felt a surge of confidence and purpose. She tucked the pouch of Moonflower petals safely into her satchel and turned to leave the cove, ready to face the next challenge on her quest.

As she made her way back to the village, the sun rising high in the sky, Elara felt a deep sense of connection to the sea and the mermaid she had vowed to save. The journey ahead would be long and arduous, but she knew that with courage, determination, and the support of her friends, she would succeed.

And so, with the first ingredient secured and the promise of more adventures to come, Elara set off toward the Mountain of Echoes, her heart filled with hope and her spirit unyielding. The mysterious voice of Seraphina echoed in her mind, a constant reminder of the bond they shared and the destiny that awaited them both.

Chapter 3: The Legend of the Sea Witch

The Calm Before the Tale

As the first light of dawn broke over the horizon, casting a golden glow on the tranquil waters of the hidden cove, Elara stood at the water's edge, the enchanted shell clutched tightly in her hands. The journey to the Whispering Woods and the acquisition of the Moonflower petals had been both challenging and enlightening, and Elara felt a renewed sense of purpose. She was determined to help Seraphina break the curse that bound her to the cove.

Seraphina emerged from the depths, her shimmering tail glinting in the early morning light. Her eyes met Elara's, filled with a mixture of gratitude and determination. "Elara, thank you for bringing the Moonflower petals," she said, her voice a melodic whisper that seemed to blend with the sound of the waves. "Now, before we continue our quest, it is time for you to understand the true nature of the curse and the one who cast it."

Elara nodded, her curiosity piqued. She settled onto a rock at the water's edge, her gaze fixed on Seraphina. "Tell me everything," she said. "I want to know who Morgana is and how she came to have such power over you."

Seraphina sighed, a wistful look in her eyes. "It is a long and tragic tale, Elara. A story of ambition, betrayal, and dark magic. But it is also a story that must be told if we are to succeed in breaking this curse."

The Rise of Morgana

"LONG AGO, IN A TIME when the boundaries between the human world and the realm of the sea were more fluid, there was a young woman named Morgana. She was born in a small fishing village, much like Marinia, but her heart was filled with a desire for something more. She was drawn to the sea, fascinated by its mysteries and the power it seemed to hold.

"Morgana possessed a rare gift—a natural affinity for magic. From a young age, she could manipulate the elements of water and air, and she often used her powers to help her village, calming storms and guiding fishermen to bountiful catches. The villagers revered her, seeing her as a blessed child, but Morgana's ambitions extended far beyond the confines of her small village.

"One fateful day, Morgana encountered a mysterious stranger on the shore. He was an ancient sea wizard named Thalor, who had long been searching for a worthy apprentice to whom he could pass on his vast knowledge. Recognizing Morgana's potential, he offered to teach her the secrets of the deep and the powerful magic that lay within it.

"Morgana eagerly accepted Thalor's offer, and under his tutelage, her powers grew exponentially. She learned to control the tides, to summon storms, and to communicate with the creatures of the sea. But with great power came a growing darkness within her. Morgana's thirst for knowledge and control became insatiable, and she began to covet the power of the sea for herself.

"Thalor, seeing the darkness in his apprentice's heart, tried to warn her of the dangers of such ambition. But Morgana would not be deterred. She betrayed Thalor, using the very magic he had taught her to bind him in an eternal sleep beneath the waves. With her mentor out of the way, Morgana proclaimed herself the Sea Witch and set out to dominate the oceans."

The Emergence of the Curse

SERAPHINA PAUSED, HER gaze distant as she recalled the ancient memories. "It was during this time that I, too, emerged as a guardian of the sea. I had always felt a deep connection to the ocean and its inhabitants, and I was chosen to protect its balance and harmony. I was young and idealistic, believing that I could counter Morgana's growing influence.

"For a while, I succeeded. I used my own powers to shield the creatures of the sea from Morgana's wrath and to maintain the natural order. But Morgana's power was vast and growing, fueled by the dark magic she had embraced. She saw me as a threat to her dominion and decided that I had to be eliminated.

"In a fierce confrontation, Morgana confronted me with her full might. The battle was long and brutal, our magic clashing in a storm of energy that shook the very foundations of the ocean. I fought with all my strength, but Morgana's power, fueled by her dark ambition, was overwhelming.

"Realizing that she could not defeat me outright, Morgana devised a crueler fate. She cast a powerful curse, binding me to this cove and stripping me of my ability to communicate freely. The enchanted shell you hold is the only means by which I can speak, and even then, my power is greatly diminished."

Seraphina's voice trembled with emotion, and Elara could see the pain and longing in her eyes. "For centuries, I have been trapped here, unable to fulfill my role as a guardian. I have watched as Morgana's influence spread, causing harm to the very world I swore to protect. But I have also seen glimpses of hope, like you, Elara—brave souls who have the potential to make a difference."

Elara's Resolve

ELARA LISTENED INTENTLY, her heart aching for Seraphina and the burden she had carried for so long. She felt a surge of anger toward Morgana and a fierce determination to break the curse and restore balance to the sea.

"Seraphina, we will find a way to break this curse," Elara said firmly. "You have been trapped and suffering for far too long. I am committed to seeing this through, no matter what challenges lie ahead."

Seraphina's eyes shone with gratitude. "Thank you, Elara. Your courage and kindness give me hope. The journey will be perilous, but together, I believe we can succeed."

Elara nodded, feeling a renewed sense of purpose. "What must we do next?"

Seraphina took a deep breath, her expression turning serious. "The second ingredient we need is the Echoing Crystals from the Mountain of Echoes. These crystals are known for their ability to amplify magic and are crucial to breaking the curse. However, the mountain is treacherous, and the crystals are guarded by powerful spirits."

Elara felt a thrill of anticipation. "Then that is where I will go next. Tell me more about these spirits and how I can obtain the crystals."

The Spirits of the Mountain

SERAPHINA'S GAZE GREW distant as she recounted the legends. "The Mountain of Echoes is a place where the veil between the physical world and the spirit realm is thin. The spirits that dwell there are ancient and powerful, guardians of the mountain's secrets. They are known as the Echoing Ones, and they have the ability to manipulate sound and vibration.

"To obtain the Echoing Crystals, you must prove yourself worthy to the Echoing Ones. They will test your resolve, your bravery, and your ability to understand the true nature of sound and silence. The journey to the mountain is perilous, and the path is fraught with challenges. But I believe in you, Elara. You have already shown great courage and determination."

Elara felt a mixture of excitement and trepidation. The journey ahead sounded daunting, but she was ready to face whatever challenges came her way. "I will prepare for the journey and leave as soon as I can," she said. "Is there anything else I should know?"

Seraphina nodded. "Take this with you," she said, holding out a small, silver pendant shaped like a seashell. "It is a charm of protection, imbued with my magic. It will help shield you from harm and guide you on your path. And remember, Elara, you are not alone. The sea and its creatures are with you, and you have the strength to overcome any obstacle."

Elara accepted the pendant with gratitude, feeling its comforting warmth in her hand. "Thank you, Seraphina. I will not let you down."

The Journey to the Mountain of Echoes

WITH SERAPHINA'S BLESSING and the pendant around her neck, Elara set out on her journey to the Mountain of Echoes. She gathered her supplies, including food, water, and the guiding stone that had led her to the Moonflowers. She also took a moment to say goodbye to her father, Finn, who wished her luck and reminded her to stay safe.

The path to the Mountain of Echoes was long and arduous, taking Elara through dense forests, across rushing rivers, and up steep, rocky slopes. As she traveled, she felt a growing sense of connection to the land and the sea, as if the very elements were watching over her and guiding her steps.

Days turned into weeks as Elara journeyed ever closer to the mountain. She encountered many challenges along the way, from fierce storms to treacherous terrain, but she persevered, driven by her determination to help Seraphina and break the curse.

Finally, after many days of travel, Elara reached the base of the Mountain of Echoes. The mountain loomed before her, its peaks shrouded in mist and its slopes covered in a dense forest of ancient trees. The air was filled with a strange, resonant hum, as if the very rocks and trees were singing a song that only the mountain could hear.

Taking a deep breath, Elara began her ascent, feeling the weight of her quest pressing down on her but also the lightness of hope and purpose.

The Trials of the Echoing Ones

AS ELARA CLIMBED HIGHER, the air grew thinner and the path steeper. The hum of the mountain grew louder, resonating in her bones and filling her with a sense of awe and reverence. She knew she was entering a sacred place, where the boundaries between the physical and the spiritual were blurred.

After hours of climbing, Elara reached a plateau where a circle of ancient stones stood, each one inscribed with intricate runes. In the center of the circle, a figure awaited her—a tall, ethereal being with translucent skin and eyes that glowed with an inner light. The Echoing One radiated an aura of power and wisdom, and Elara felt a mixture of fear and respect as she approached.

"Welcome, Elara," the Echoing One said, its voice a harmonious blend of many tones. "We have been expecting you. You seek the Echoing Crystals to break a curse, but first, you must prove yourself worthy."

Elara nodded, her resolve unwavering. "I am ready to face any challenge," she said.

The Echoing One raised its hand, and the air around Elara began to shimmer with energy. "Your first trial is the Trial of Sound," the Echoing One said. "You must navigate the Maze of Echoes, where every sound you make will be amplified and turned against you. Silence and clarity of mind will guide you through."

With those words, the ground beneath Elara's feet shifted, and she found herself standing at the entrance of a labyrinth made of shimmering, translucent walls. The walls vibrated with a low hum, and Elara knew that even the slightest noise would be magnified within the maze.

Taking a deep breath, Elara stepped into the maze, her heart pounding with anticipation. She moved slowly and carefully, mindful of every step and breath.

The walls seemed to pulse with energy, and she could hear the faint echoes of her own movements reverberating around her.

As she navigated the maze, Elara encountered various challenges designed to test her resolve. Sudden gusts of wind would rustle the leaves, creating a cacophony of sound. The ground would shift beneath her feet, causing her to stumble. But through it all, Elara remained focused, using her inner strength to maintain her composure and silence.

Finally, after what felt like hours, Elara reached the center of the maze, where a small, glowing crystal awaited her. She picked it up, feeling its warmth and energy flow through her. The walls of the maze dissolved, and she found herself back in the circle of stones, facing the Echoing One.

"You have passed the Trial of Sound," the Echoing One said, its voice filled with approval. "Now you must face the Trial of Silence. You will be taken to the Cavern of Silence, where all sound is absorbed. In the silence, you must find the hidden crystal, guided only by your intuition and inner light."

The ground shifted again, and Elara found herself standing at the entrance of a dark cavern. The air inside was heavy and still, as if the very essence of sound had been stripped away. She stepped into the cavern, feeling the silence envelop her like a thick blanket.

In the absence of sound, Elara relied on her other senses. She moved slowly and deliberately, her eyes scanning the darkness for any sign of the crystal. The pendant around her neck glowed faintly, providing a small source of light and guidance.

As she ventured deeper into the cavern, Elara felt a growing sense of calm and clarity. The silence allowed her to connect with her inner self, to listen to her own thoughts and feelings without distraction. She followed her intuition, trusting that it would lead her to the hidden crystal.

After what felt like an eternity, Elara saw a faint glimmer of light in the darkness. She approached it cautiously, her heart pounding with anticipation. There, nestled in a small crevice in the rock, was the second Echoing Crystal. She reached out and took it, feeling a sense of triumph and relief.

The cavern dissolved around her, and Elara found herself back in the circle of stones, facing the Echoing One once more.

"You have passed the Trial of Silence," the Echoing One said, its voice filled with pride. "You have proven your worthiness and shown that you possess the qualities needed to wield the Echoing Crystals. They are yours to take."

With a gesture, the Echoing One presented Elara with a pouch containing several glowing crystals. She accepted them with gratitude, feeling their power and energy resonate with her own.

Returning to Seraphina

WITH THE ECHOING CRYSTALS in hand, Elara began her descent from the Mountain of Echoes. The journey back to the hidden cove was long and challenging, but Elara felt a renewed sense of purpose and determination. She had faced her trials and emerged victorious, and she was eager to share her success with Seraphina.

As she approached the cove, Elara saw Seraphina waiting for her, a look of hopeful anticipation in her eyes. Elara knelt at the water's edge and held out the pouch of Echoing Crystals.

"I have the crystals, Seraphina," she said, her voice filled with pride. "What do we do next?"

Seraphina's eyes sparkled with gratitude and relief. "Thank you, Elara. The second ingredient is ours. Now we must gather the Golden Seaweed from the Sunken Ruins. It will be a difficult journey, but I have faith in you."

Elara nodded, feeling a renewed sense of determination. "I will head to the Sunken Ruins at once. We will break this curse, Seraphina. I promise."

Seraphina smiled, her eyes shining with hope. "I know you will, Elara. You are a true friend and a brave soul. The sea is with you, always."

With those words, Elara felt a surge of confidence and purpose. She tucked the pouch of Echoing Crystals safely into her satchel and turned to leave the cove, ready to face the next challenge on her quest.

As she made her way back to the village, the sun rising high in the sky, Elara felt a deep sense of connection to the sea and the mermaid she had vowed to save. The journey ahead would be long and arduous, but she knew that with courage, determination, and the support of her friends, she would succeed.

And so, with the second ingredient secured and the promise of more adventures to come, Elara set off toward the Sunken Ruins, her heart filled with hope and her spirit unyielding. The legend of Morgana and the curse that bound Seraphina continued to drive her forward, a reminder of the bond they shared and the destiny that awaited them both.

Chapter 4: The Quest Begins

The Journey's Inception

The morning sun had just begun to creep over the horizon, casting a soft, golden light on the village of Marinia. The air was filled with the familiar scent of salt and seaweed, a comforting reminder of the ocean's presence. Elara stood at the edge of the village, her heart pounding with a mixture of excitement and trepidation. Today was the day her journey would truly begin.

The Moonflower petals and the Echoing Crystals had been obtained, but the path ahead was still long and fraught with challenges. Seraphina's curse was a heavy burden, and Elara felt the weight of responsibility pressing down on her shoulders. But she also felt a sense of purpose, a determination to see this quest through to the end.

Elara's father, Finn, stood beside her, his weathered face filled with pride and concern. "Remember, Elara," he said, his voice steady, "the sea is both friend and foe. Trust your instincts, and don't be afraid to ask for help when you need it."

Elara nodded, hugging her father tightly. "I will, Father. Thank you for believing in me."

With her satchel packed and the enchanted shell safely tucked inside, Elara set off towards the home of Maelis, the village elder. Maelis had always been a source of wisdom and guidance for the people of Marinia, and Elara knew she would need the elder's insight to find the remaining ingredients for the potion.

Seeking the Village Elder's Guidance

MAELIS LIVED IN A SMALL, charming cottage on the outskirts of the village, surrounded by a lush garden filled with herbs, flowers, and ancient trees. The scent of lavender and rosemary filled the air, creating a sense of calm and tranquility. As Elara approached the cottage, she felt a surge of hope. Maelis had always been kind to her, and she trusted the elder's knowledge implicitly.

Elara knocked gently on the wooden door, and after a moment, it swung open to reveal Maelis, her silver hair cascading down her back and her eyes twinkling with curiosity. "Elara, my dear," she said warmly, "I've been expecting you. Come in, come in."

Elara stepped inside, taking in the familiar surroundings. The cottage was filled with shelves of books, jars of herbs, and curious trinkets from Maelis's travels. A large, oak table in the center of the room held an assortment of maps and scrolls.

"Thank you for seeing me, Maelis," Elara said, her voice tinged with both excitement and urgency. "I need your help to find the ingredients to break Seraphina's curse."

Maelis nodded, her expression serious. "I know, Elara. The sea has whispered to me of your quest. You have already shown great courage and determination, but the path ahead will not be easy. Come, let us sit and discuss what you need."

Elara followed Maelis to the table, where the elder spread out a large, ancient map. The map was intricately detailed, depicting the lands and seas surrounding Marinia, along with various symbols and markings indicating places of significance.

"The ingredients you seek are rare and protected by powerful forces," Maelis explained. "The Moonflower petals and the Echoing Crystals were just the beginning. You still need the Golden Seaweed from the Sunken Ruins and the Shadow Berries from the Island of Shadows."

Elara listened intently, her eyes scanning the map. "Where do I start?" she asked.

The First Destination: The Whispering Woods

MAELIS POINTED TO A dense forest marked on the map, labeled as the Whispering Woods. "Your first destination is the Whispering Woods. It is a place of ancient magic, where the trees seem to whisper secrets to those who listen. The Moonflower petals you seek grow deep within the forest, but they are protected by the guardian of the woods, Lyria."

Elara nodded, recalling her previous encounter with Lyria and the trials she had faced to obtain the Moonflower petals. "I remember the trials," she said softly. "It was a test of courage and purity of heart."

"Indeed," Maelis agreed. "And you passed with flying colors. But the woods hold more secrets and challenges. Lyria is a wise and fair guardian, but she will test you again to ensure you are worthy of the next stage of your journey."

Elara felt a surge of determination. "I am ready to face whatever challenges come my way," she said firmly.

Maelis smiled, her eyes filled with pride. "I have no doubt you will succeed, Elara. Take this map with you, and these herbs," she said, handing Elara a small pouch filled with dried leaves and flowers. "They will provide you with protection and strength. And remember, the sea is always with you."

Elara accepted the map and the herbs with gratitude, feeling a renewed sense of confidence. "Thank you, Maelis. I will return with the ingredients."

With the map securely in her satchel, Elara set off towards the Whispering Woods, her heart filled with a mixture of anticipation and resolve.

Entering the Whispering Woods

THE WHISPERING WOODS lay to the north of Marinia, a dense forest known for its towering trees and the eerie whispers that filled the air. The villagers spoke of the woods with a mixture of reverence and caution, for while they were a place of beauty and wonder, they also held secrets and dangers.

As Elara approached the edge of the forest, she felt a shiver of excitement and trepidation. The trees towered above her, their branches forming a thick canopy that filtered the sunlight into a soft, green glow. She could hear the faint whisper of leaves rustling in the breeze, a sound that seemed almost like voices murmuring just beyond her hearing.

Taking a deep breath, Elara stepped into the woods, feeling the cool, mossy ground beneath her feet. She reached into her satchel and pulled out the guiding stone, holding it in her palm. The stone glowed with a soft, ethereal light, pulsing gently as if in tune with her heartbeat.

Elara followed the stone's light, moving deeper into the forest. The trees seemed to close in around her, their whispers growing louder and more distinct.

She could almost make out words, but they remained just beyond her understanding, like a song sung in a language she didn't know.

As she walked, Elara felt a growing sense of unease. The forest was beautiful, but it was also unsettling, as if it were watching her, judging her worthiness. She reminded herself of Seraphina's words and the importance of her quest, using her determination to push through her fear.

The Guardians of the Moonflowers

AFTER HOURS OF WALKING, the guiding stone's light grew brighter, signaling that she was getting closer to the Moonflowers. Elara's spirits lifted, and she quickened her pace, eager to complete the first part of her journey.

Eventually, she came upon a small clearing bathed in a soft, silver light. In the center of the clearing grew a cluster of Moonflowers, their petals glowing with a pale, otherworldly luminescence. Elara approached the flowers with reverence, marveling at their delicate beauty.

Just as she was about to pick the first petal, a voice rang out, clear and commanding. "Who dares to disturb the Moonflowers?"

Elara froze, her heart pounding. She turned to see a figure step out from the shadows of the trees. It was Lyria, the guardian of the Whispering Woods, her tall and regal form illuminated by the moonlight.

"I am Elara," she said, her voice steady despite her fear. "I seek the Moonflower petals to break a curse and free a mermaid named Seraphina."

Lyria studied her for a moment, her expression unreadable. "I remember you, Elara. You have proven your courage and purity of heart before. But the woods hold more challenges, and the path ahead is fraught with danger. Are you prepared to face the trials once more?"

Elara nodded, her resolve unwavering. "I am ready."

Lyria raised her hands, and the clearing began to shimmer with magic. "Your test is this: You must navigate the Maze of Reflections once more, and face the trials of sound and silence. Only by overcoming these challenges can you prove your worthiness."

With those words, the ground beneath Elara's feet shifted, and she found herself standing at the entrance of a labyrinth made of shimmering mirrors. The walls of the maze reflected her image back at her from every angle, creating a dizzying effect.

Taking a deep breath, Elara stepped into the maze, her heart pounding with a mixture of fear and determination. She knew that this test would not be easy, but she also knew that she could not fail. Seraphina was counting on her.

The Maze of Reflections

AS ELARA WALKED DEEPER into the maze, she felt a growing sense of unease. The mirrors reflected not just her physical appearance, but also her thoughts and emotions. She saw herself as a child, grieving the loss of her mother. She saw the moments of doubt and insecurity that had plagued her over the years. Each reflection seemed to taunt her, highlighting her fears and weaknesses.

Elara forced herself to keep moving, refusing to be paralyzed by her own reflections. She reminded herself of the strength and courage that had brought her this far. She had faced loss and hardship before, and she would not be defeated by her own mind.

As she navigated the maze, Elara encountered reflections that seemed to speak to her, their voices echoing in her mind.

"You're not strong enough," one reflection whispered.

"You'll never succeed," another taunted.

Elara clenched her fists, fighting back the tears that threatened to spill over. "I am strong enough," she said aloud, her voice echoing in the maze. "I will succeed."

With each step, she felt her resolve strengthen. She began to focus on the positive reflections, the moments of courage and determination that had defined her. She saw herself standing up to bullies as a child, comforting her father during difficult times, and embarking on this quest with unwavering determination.

Slowly but surely, the negative reflections began to fade, replaced by images of strength and resilience. Elara felt a sense of clarity and peace wash over her, as if a weight had been lifted from her shoulders.

Finally, she reached the center of the maze, where a single, clear mirror stood. In its reflection, she saw herself as she truly was—strong, brave, and determined. She smiled, feeling a surge of pride and confidence.

"You have passed the test," Lyria's voice echoed through the maze. "You have proven your courage and purity of heart."

The maze dissolved around her, and Elara found herself back in the clearing, standing before Lyria. The guardian smiled warmly and handed her a small pouch filled with Moonflower petals.

"You have earned these, Elara," Lyria said. "May they help you in your quest to free Seraphina."

Elara accepted the pouch with gratitude, her heart swelling with pride. "Thank you, Lyria. I will not forget your kindness."

Returning to Seraphina

WITH THE MOONFLOWER petals in hand, Elara made her way back to the hidden cove. The journey through the Whispering Woods had been challenging, but it had also strengthened her resolve and deepened her understanding of her own strength.

As she approached the cove, she saw Seraphina waiting for her, a look of hopeful anticipation in her eyes. Elara knelt at the water's edge and held out the pouch of Moonflower petals.

"I have the petals, Seraphina," she said, her voice filled with pride. "What do we do next?"

Seraphina's eyes sparkled with gratitude and relief. "Thank you, Elara. The first ingredient is ours. Now we must gather the Echoing Crystals from the Mountain of Echoes. It will be a difficult journey, but I have faith in you."

Elara nodded, feeling a renewed sense of determination. "I will head to the mountain at once. We will break this curse, Seraphina. I promise."

Seraphina smiled, her eyes shining with hope. "I know you will, Elara. You are a true friend and a brave soul. The sea is with you, always."

With those words, Elara felt a surge of confidence and purpose. She tucked the pouch of Moonflower petals safely into her satchel and turned to leave the cove, ready to face the next challenge on her quest.

As she made her way back to the village, the sun rising high in the sky, Elara felt a deep sense of connection to the sea and the mermaid she had vowed to save. The journey ahead would be long and arduous, but she knew that with courage, determination, and the support of her friends, she would succeed.

And so, with the first ingredient secured and the promise of more adventures to come, Elara set off toward the Mountain of Echoes, her heart filled with hope and her spirit unyielding. The mysterious voice of Seraphina echoed in her mind, a constant reminder of the bond they shared and the destiny that awaited them both.

Chapter 5: The Whispering Woods

Entering the Whispering Woods

The Whispering Woods loomed ahead, a dense forest known for its ancient magic and hidden secrets. Elara had visited these woods once before, but this time felt different. The journey ahead promised new challenges, and she was determined to succeed for Seraphina's sake.

Elara paused at the edge of the forest, taking a deep breath to steady her nerves. The tall trees formed a thick canopy, casting the forest floor in a perpetual twilight. The air was filled with the sounds of rustling leaves and distant whispers, as if the woods themselves were alive, murmuring secrets just beyond her hearing.

Clutching the map Maelis had given her, Elara took her first steps into the forest. The path was narrow and overgrown, but the guiding stone in her satchel glowed softly, providing a sense of direction and comfort. She followed the stone's light, moving deeper into the woods, her senses alert for any sign of danger or opportunity.

Encounter with Mythical Creatures

AS ELARA VENTURED FURTHER, the forest seemed to close in around her. The trees grew taller and more imposing, their branches twisting together like the arms of ancient guardians. The whispers grew louder, forming a symphony of voices that filled her mind with a sense of wonder and trepidation.

After several hours of walking, Elara came upon a clearing bathed in a soft, golden light. In the center of the clearing stood a majestic stag with antlers that seemed to shimmer with an ethereal glow. The stag watched her with intelligent eyes, its presence both serene and commanding.

Elara approached cautiously, her heart pounding with excitement. "Hello," she said softly, not wanting to startle the creature. "My name is Elara. I'm on a quest to gather ingredients to break a curse. Can you help me?"

The stag regarded her for a moment, then dipped its head in a gesture of acknowledgment. "Greetings, Elara," it said, its voice resonant and calming. "I am Eldrin, the guardian of this part of the forest. The woods have spoken of your quest. What is it that you seek?"

Elara explained her mission, describing the Moonflower petals and their importance to breaking Seraphina's curse. Eldrin listened attentively, his expression thoughtful.

"The Moonflower petals are indeed powerful," Eldrin said. "But they are protected by the guardian of the woods, Lyria. To obtain them, you must prove your worthiness. The path to the Moonflowers is fraught with challenges, and you will need guidance to navigate it."

Elara nodded, her resolve firm. "I am ready to face any challenge. Can you guide me to the Moonflowers, Eldrin?"

The stag shook his head. "I cannot leave my post, but I can send you a guide. Orin, come forth."

From the shadows of the trees, a small, brown owl with striking golden eyes fluttered into view. The owl perched on a low branch, regarding Elara with a curious tilt of its head.

"This is Orin," Eldrin said. "He is wise and knowledgeable about the forest. He will guide you to the Moonflowers and help you navigate the challenges ahead."

Orin hooted softly, his eyes twinkling with intelligence. "Greetings, Elara," he said in a melodic voice. "It will be my honor to guide you. The Whispering Woods are filled with wonders and dangers, but together, we will succeed."

Elara smiled, feeling a surge of hope. "Thank you, Orin. I'm glad to have you by my side."

With Orin leading the way, Elara continued her journey through the forest, her spirits lifted by the presence of her new companion.

Navigating the Forest's Challenges

THE PATH THROUGH THE Whispering Woods was winding and treacherous, but Orin's guidance proved invaluable. The owl flew ahead, perching on branches and calling out directions, his keen eyes spotting obstacles and hidden dangers before they could pose a threat.

As they traveled, Elara marveled at the beauty of the forest. The trees were ancient and majestic, their branches forming intricate patterns against the sky. The ground was carpeted with soft moss and delicate wildflowers, and the air was filled with the sweet scent of blooming plants.

But the forest was also filled with challenges. At one point, they came upon a wide, rushing river with no visible way to cross. The water was deep and fast-moving, its surface glinting in the dappled sunlight.

"We need to find a way across," Elara said, scanning the riverbank for any sign of a bridge or shallow spot.

Orin hooted thoughtfully. "There is a narrow bridge further upstream, but it is guarded by a mischievous sprite named Lirien. She loves to play tricks on travelers, but if you can win her favor, she will allow us to cross."

Elara nodded, determined to face whatever lay ahead. "Lead the way, Orin."

They followed the river upstream until they reached a narrow, rickety bridge spanning the water. As they approached, a small, ethereal figure materialized on the bridge. Lirien had delicate wings that shimmered with a rainbow of colors and a mischievous smile that played across her lips.

"Who dares to cross my bridge?" Lirien called out, her voice lilting and playful.

"I am Elara, and this is Orin," Elara replied. "We seek passage across the river. Can you help us?"

Lirien fluttered closer, her eyes twinkling with mischief. "Perhaps. But first, you must solve my riddle. If you answer correctly, I will let you pass. If not, you must turn back."

Elara nodded, ready to face the challenge. "Ask your riddle, Lirien."

The sprite's smile widened, and she recited the riddle in a sing-song voice:

"I speak without a mouth and hear without ears. I have no body, but I come alive with wind. What am I?"

Elara thought for a moment, her mind racing. She had heard this riddle before, in one of the stories her father used to tell her. The answer came to her in a flash of insight.

"An echo," she said confidently. "The answer is an echo."

Lirien's eyes widened in surprise, and then she burst into laughter. "Well done, Elara! You have answered correctly. You may cross my bridge."

With a graceful gesture, Lirien beckoned them forward. Elara and Orin carefully crossed the narrow bridge, grateful for the sprite's guidance.

The Guardians of the Moonflowers

WITH THE RIVER BEHIND them, Elara and Orin continued their journey deeper into the forest. The guiding stone's light grew brighter, signaling that they were getting closer to the Moonflowers. Elara's spirits lifted, knowing that they were making progress.

As they approached a dense thicket, Orin hooted softly, signaling Elara to stop. "The Moonflowers are just beyond this thicket," he said. "But be cautious. Lyria, the guardian of the woods, will test you before allowing you to take the petals."

Elara nodded, steeling herself for the challenge ahead. She pushed through the thicket, emerging into a small clearing bathed in a soft, silver light. In the center of the clearing grew a cluster of Moonflowers, their petals glowing with an otherworldly luminescence.

Just as Elara reached out to pick a petal, a figure materialized before her. It was Lyria, the guardian of the Whispering Woods, her tall and regal form illuminated by the moonlight.

"Elara," Lyria said, her voice calm and commanding. "You have come for the Moonflower petals. But before you can take them, you must prove your worthiness once more."

Elara nodded, her resolve unwavering. "I am ready to face any challenge."

Lyria raised her hands, and the clearing began to shimmer with magic. "Your test is this: You must navigate the Maze of Reflections and face the trials of sound and silence. Only by overcoming these challenges can you prove your worthiness."

With those words, the ground beneath Elara's feet shifted, and she found herself standing at the entrance of a labyrinth made of shimmering mirrors. The walls of the maze reflected her image back at her from every angle, creating a dizzying effect.

The Maze of Reflections

AS ELARA WALKED DEEPER into the maze, she felt a growing sense of unease. The mirrors reflected not just her physical appearance, but also her thoughts and emotions. She saw herself as a child, grieving the loss of her mother. She saw the moments of doubt and insecurity that had plagued her over the years. Each reflection seemed to taunt her, highlighting her fears and weaknesses.

Elara forced herself to keep moving, refusing to be paralyzed by her own reflections. She reminded herself of the strength and courage that had brought her this far. She had faced loss and hardship before, and she would not be defeated by her own mind.

As she navigated the maze, Elara encountered reflections that seemed to speak to her, their voices echoing in her mind.

"You're not strong enough," one reflection whispered.

"You'll never succeed," another taunted.

Elara clenched her fists, fighting back the tears that threatened to spill over. "I am strong enough," she said aloud, her voice echoing in the maze. "I will succeed."

With each step, she felt her resolve strengthen. She began to focus on the positive reflections, the moments of courage and determination that had defined her. She saw herself standing up to bullies as a child, comforting her father during difficult times, and embarking on this quest with unwavering determination

.

Slowly but surely, the negative reflections began to fade, replaced by images of strength and resilience. Elara felt a sense of clarity and peace wash over her, as if a weight had been lifted from her shoulders.

Finally, she reached the center of the maze, where a single, clear mirror stood. In its reflection, she saw herself as she truly was—strong, brave, and determined. She smiled, feeling a surge of pride and confidence.

"You have passed the test," Lyria's voice echoed through the maze. "You have proven your courage and purity of heart."

The maze dissolved around her, and Elara found herself back in the clearing, standing before Lyria. The guardian smiled warmly and handed her a small pouch filled with Moonflower petals.

"You have earned these, Elara," Lyria said. "May they help you in your quest to free Seraphina."

Elara accepted the pouch with gratitude, her heart swelling with pride. "Thank you, Lyria. I will not forget your kindness."

Orin's Guidance

WITH THE MOONFLOWER petals in hand, Elara felt a renewed sense of hope and determination. Orin fluttered down to perch on her shoulder, his golden eyes filled with pride.

"You did well, Elara," Orin said. "Lyria's tests are not easy, but you faced them with courage and grace."

Elara smiled, feeling a deep sense of connection to her new friend. "Thank you, Orin. I couldn't have done it without your guidance."

Orin hooted softly, a sound that seemed to convey both comfort and encouragement. "The journey is far from over, but together, we will succeed."

With Orin leading the way, Elara began the journey back to the hidden cove, eager to share her success with Seraphina and to continue their quest.

Return to the Hidden Cove

THE JOURNEY BACK TO the hidden cove was filled with a sense of accomplishment and anticipation. The forest seemed less daunting now, its whispers more welcoming than before. Elara felt a newfound connection to the Whispering Woods, as if the forest itself had accepted her as a worthy ally.

As they approached the cove, Elara saw Seraphina waiting for her, a look of hopeful anticipation in her eyes. Elara knelt at the water's edge and held out the pouch of Moonflower petals.

"I have the petals, Seraphina," she said, her voice filled with pride. "What do we do next?"

Seraphina's eyes sparkled with gratitude and relief. "Thank you, Elara. The first ingredient is ours. Now we must gather the Echoing Crystals from the Mountain of Echoes. It will be a difficult journey, but I have faith in you."

Elara nodded, feeling a renewed sense of determination. "I will head to the mountain at once. We will break this curse, Seraphina. I promise."

Seraphina smiled, her eyes shining with hope. "I know you will, Elara. You are a true friend and a brave soul. The sea is with you, always."

With those words, Elara felt a surge of confidence and purpose. She tucked the pouch of Moonflower petals safely into her satchel and turned to leave the cove, ready to face the next challenge on her quest.

As she made her way back to the village, the sun rising high in the sky, Elara felt a deep sense of connection to the sea and the mermaid she had vowed to save. The journey ahead would be long and arduous, but she knew that with courage, determination, and the support of her friends, she would succeed.

And so, with the first ingredient secured and the promise of more adventures to come, Elara set off toward the Mountain of Echoes, her heart filled with hope and her spirit unyielding. The mysterious voice of Seraphina echoed in her mind, a constant reminder of the bond they shared and the destiny that awaited them both.

Chapter 6: The Mountain of Echoes

Setting Out for the Mountain

Elara stood at the edge of the village, her eyes fixed on the distant peaks of the Mountain of Echoes. The journey to the Whispering Woods had tested her resolve and strengthened her spirit, but she knew that the climb ahead would be even more challenging. The Echoing Crystals, the second ingredient needed to break Seraphina's curse, awaited her at the summit. With the enchanted shell and the Moonflower petals safely tucked in her satchel, Elara felt a mixture of determination and trepidation.

Orin, the talking owl who had guided her through the Whispering Woods, perched on her shoulder, his golden eyes filled with wisdom and encouragement. "The Mountain of Echoes is a place of great power and mystery," he said. "The path is treacherous, and the trials you will face are unlike any you have encountered before. But remember, Elara, you are not alone. I will be with you every step of the way."

Elara nodded, her resolve firm. "Thank you, Orin. I'm ready to face whatever lies ahead. We need those crystals to free Seraphina, and I won't let anything stop us."

With a final glance back at the village, Elara set off toward the mountain, her heart filled with hope and determination.

The Ascent Begins

THE JOURNEY TO THE base of the mountain took several days, during which Elara and Orin traversed rugged terrain and crossed swift-flowing rivers. As they drew closer to their destination, the landscape grew more barren and rocky, the air thinner and colder. The Mountain of Echoes loomed ahead, its peaks shrouded in mist, and the resonant hum that filled the air grew louder, vibrating through Elara's very bones.

On the morning of their ascent, Elara stood at the base of the mountain, gazing up at the steep, winding path that lay before them. The trail was narrow and treacherous, cutting through jagged rocks and dense underbrush. The echoes of distant sounds reverberated through the air, creating an eerie symphony that both intrigued and unnerved her.

"Are you ready, Elara?" Orin asked, his voice gentle but firm.

Elara took a deep breath, her gaze resolute. "I'm ready. Let's do this."

With Orin guiding her from above, Elara began the arduous climb. The path was steep and uneven, forcing her to navigate carefully to avoid slipping on loose rocks or losing her footing on the narrow ledges. The higher they climbed, the colder the air became, and the mist grew thicker, obscuring her vision and adding to the sense of isolation.

Despite the challenges, Elara pressed on, driven by her determination to retrieve the Echoing Crystals and break Seraphina's curse. Each step brought her closer to her goal, and she drew strength from Orin's presence and the knowledge that she was not alone.

Trials of Sound

AS ELARA AND ORIN ASCENDED the mountain, they reached a plateau where the path widened into a broad, open space. The air was filled with a resonant hum, and the ground beneath their feet seemed to vibrate with an unseen energy. Elara could feel the power of the mountain all around her, a palpable force that both awed and intimidated her.

At the center of the plateau stood a series of tall, stone pillars arranged in a circular pattern. The pillars were covered in intricate carvings, and at their base lay a shimmering pool of water, its surface perfectly still. Elara knew instinctively that this was the first trial—the Trial of Sound.

Orin fluttered down to perch on one of the pillars, his eyes filled with solemnity. "This is the first trial, Elara," he said. "The Echoing Ones, the spirits of the mountain, will test your ability to understand and manipulate sound. You must use your voice to create harmony and balance. Only then will the path forward be revealed."

Elara approached the center of the circle, her heart pounding with anticipation. She closed her eyes and took a deep breath, focusing on the sounds around her—the hum of the mountain, the rustling of the wind, and the distant echoes of her own footsteps. She began to hum softly, her voice blending with the natural symphony of the mountain.

As she hummed, the air around her seemed to vibrate in response, the stone pillars resonating with her voice. She increased the volume, letting her voice rise and fall in a melodic pattern, seeking the perfect harmony that would unlock the path forward. The pillars began to glow with a soft, ethereal light, and the shimmering pool of water rippled gently.

Elara continued to sing, her voice growing stronger and more confident. She let the echoes guide her, following their lead as she wove a tapestry of sound that filled the plateau with a sense of peace and balance. The light from the pillars intensified, and the ripples in the pool grew more pronounced, forming intricate patterns on the surface.

Finally, with a final, soaring note, Elara felt a surge of energy course through her. The pillars blazed with light, and the pool of water shimmered like a mirror. The echoes around her grew louder, forming a harmonious chorus that filled the air with a sense of completion and triumph.

The light from the pillars converged at the center of the circle, forming a glowing pathway that led upward. Elara opened her eyes, her heart filled with a sense of accomplishment and wonder.

"You have passed the Trial of Sound," Orin said, his voice filled with pride. "The Echoing Ones have acknowledged your harmony and balance. The path forward is open."

Elara smiled, feeling a renewed sense of confidence. "Thank you, Orin. Let's keep moving."

With the glowing pathway lighting their way, Elara and Orin continued their ascent, the echoes of their success resonating in their hearts.

Trials of Silence

AS THEY CLIMBED HIGHER, the air grew colder and thinner, and the path became steeper and more treacherous. The mist thickened, obscuring their vision and adding to the sense of isolation. Despite the challenges, Elara pressed on, driven by her determination to retrieve the Echoing Crystals and break Seraphina's curse.

Eventually, they reached a narrow ledge that jutted out over a deep chasm. The ledge was lined with jagged rocks, and the air was filled with a profound, eerie silence. Elara knew instinctively that this was the second trial—the Trial of Silence.

Orin perched on a nearby rock, his eyes filled with solemnity. "This is the second trial, Elara," he said. "The Echoing Ones will test your ability to understand and navigate silence. You must find the hidden path without making a sound. Trust your intuition and inner strength."

Elara nodded, her resolve firm. She took a deep breath, focusing on the silence around her. The absence of sound was disorienting, but she knew she had to remain calm and centered. She stepped onto the ledge, moving carefully to avoid dislodging any rocks or making any noise.

As she navigated the narrow path, Elara felt a growing sense of isolation. The silence was oppressive, pressing down on her like a physical weight. She could feel her own heartbeat, loud and rhythmic, and she knew that any sound could disrupt the delicate balance of the trial.

She moved slowly and deliberately, trusting her intuition to guide her. The path was treacherous, with jagged rocks and narrow ledges that required careful navigation. Elara felt her way forward, her senses heightened by the silence and the weight of the trial.

At one point, she stumbled, nearly losing her footing on a loose rock. Her heart pounded with fear, but she caught herself, steadying her balance and continuing forward. She knew she couldn't afford any mistakes—the silence was absolute, and even the slightest noise could spell disaster.

After what felt like an eternity, Elara reached the end of the ledge, where a narrow, hidden pathway led upward. The path was shrouded in mist, but she could feel its presence, a faint glimmer of hope in the oppressive silence.

She took a deep breath, focusing on her inner strength and determination. With careful, deliberate steps, she followed the hidden path, trusting her intuition to guide her. The silence seemed to grow heavier with each step, but Elara pressed on, her resolve unyielding.

Finally, after a long and arduous climb, Elara emerged onto a broad, open plateau bathed in a soft, ethereal light. The air was filled with a sense of peace and serenity, and the oppressive silence lifted, replaced by a gentle hum that resonated with her very soul.

"You have passed the Trial of Silence," Orin said, his voice filled with pride. "The Echoing Ones have acknowledged your inner strength and intuition. The path forward is open."

Elara smiled, feeling a deep sense of accomplishment and relief. "Thank you, Orin. Let's keep moving."

With the path forward illuminated by the ethereal light, Elara and Orin continued their ascent, the echoes of their success resonating in their hearts.

The Summit and the Echoing Crystals

THE FINAL LEG OF THEIR journey was the most challenging. The path grew steeper and more treacherous, the air thinner and colder. The mist thickened, obscuring their vision and adding to the sense of isolation. Despite the challenges, Elara pressed on, driven by her determination to retrieve the Echoing Crystals and break Seraphina's curse.

After hours of climbing, they reached the summit of the Mountain of Echoes. The peak was a broad, flat expanse covered in a layer of shimmering ice. At the center of the summit stood a cluster of crystal

formations, their surfaces glinting with an ethereal light. Elara knew instinctively that these were the Echoing Crystals.

As she approached the crystals, a figure materialized before her. It was an ethereal being with translucent skin and eyes that glowed with an inner light—the Echoing One. The spirit radiated an aura of power and wisdom, and Elara felt a mixture of fear and respect as she approached.

"Welcome, Elara," the Echoing One said, its voice a harmonious blend of many tones. "You have proven your worthiness by passing the Trials of Sound and Silence. The Echoing Crystals are yours to take."

Elara knelt before the crystals, her heart filled with awe and gratitude. She reached out and touched the largest crystal, feeling its warmth and energy flow through her. The crystal glowed brighter, resonating with her own inner light.

With careful, deliberate movements, Elara extracted several of the Echoing Crystals, placing them in a small pouch. The crystals hummed softly, their energy filling the air with a sense of peace and harmony.

"Thank you," Elara said, her voice filled with reverence. "I will use these crystals to break the curse and free Seraphina."

The Echoing One smiled, its eyes filled with approval. "You have shown great courage and determination, Elara. The Echoing Crystals will aid you in your quest. May your journey be filled with light and harmony."

With the Echoing Crystals safely in her satchel, Elara and Orin began their descent from the mountain. The journey down was no less challenging, but the knowledge that they had succeeded filled Elara with a sense of accomplishment and hope.

Return to the Hidden Cove

AS THEY DESCENDED THE mountain, the air grew warmer and the mist began to dissipate. The path became less treacherous, and Elara felt a renewed sense of confidence and determination. She had retrieved the Echoing Crystals, and the next step in their quest was within reach.

After several days of travel, Elara and Orin reached the base of the mountain and began the journey back to the hidden cove. The forest seemed less daunting now, its whispers more welcoming than before. Elara felt a newfound connection to the land and the spirits that inhabited it.

As they approached the cove, Elara saw Seraphina waiting for her, a look of hopeful anticipation in her eyes. Elara knelt at the water's edge and held out the pouch of Echoing Crystals.

"I have the crystals, Seraphina," she said, her voice filled with pride. "What do we do next?"

Seraphina's eyes sparkled with gratitude and relief. "Thank you, Elara. The second ingredient is ours. Now we must gather the Golden Seaweed from the Sunken Ruins. It will be a difficult journey, but I have faith in you."

Elara nodded, feeling a renewed sense of determination. "I will head to the Sunken Ruins at once. We will break this curse, Seraphina. I promise."

Seraphina smiled, her eyes shining with hope. "I know you will, Elara. You are a true friend and a brave soul. The sea is with you, always."

With those words, Elara felt a surge of confidence and purpose. She tucked the pouch of Echoing Crystals safely into her satchel and turned to leave the cove, ready to face the next challenge on her quest.

Journey to the Sunken Ruins

THE JOURNEY TO THE Sunken Ruins took Elara and Orin through dense forests, across rushing rivers, and over rugged terrain. The landscape was ever-changing, filled with both beauty and danger. Despite the challenges, Elara pressed on, driven by her determination to retrieve the Golden Seaweed and break Seraphina's curse.

As they traveled, Elara and Orin encountered various mythical creatures and faced numerous challenges. Each obstacle tested their resolve and strengthened their bond, forging a deep sense of trust and friendship between them.

Finally, after many days of travel, they reached the coast where the Sunken Ruins lay hidden beneath the waves. The ocean stretched out before them, vast and mysterious, its surface glinting in the sunlight.

Elara stood at the water's edge, her heart filled with anticipation and determination. The journey ahead would be treacherous, but she was ready to face whatever challenges came her way.

With Orin by her side and the guidance of the enchanted shell, Elara prepared to dive into the depths of the ocean and retrieve the Golden Seaweed from the Sunken Ruins. The echoes of her success on the Mountain of Echoes resonated in her heart, a constant reminder of the bond she shared with Seraphina and the destiny that awaited them both.

And so, with the second ingredient secured and the promise of more adventures to come, Elara set off toward the Sunken Ruins, her heart filled with hope and her spirit unyielding. The mysterious voice of Seraphina echoed in her mind, a constant reminder of the bond they shared and the destiny that awaited them both.

Chapter 7: The Sunken Ruins

The Journey to the Coast

The journey from the Mountain of Echoes to the coastal region where the Sunken Ruins lay hidden beneath the waves was long and arduous. Elara and Orin navigated through dense forests, crossed swift rivers, and trekked over rocky terrain. As they approached the coastline, the air grew salty, and the sound of crashing waves became a constant backdrop to their travels.

Elara felt a mixture of anticipation and trepidation. The Sunken Ruins were a place of mystery and danger, filled with ancient secrets and powerful sea creatures. She knew that retrieving the Golden Seaweed would not be easy, but she was determined to succeed. Seraphina's freedom depended on it.

Orin flew ahead, his keen eyes scanning the horizon. "We are close, Elara," he said, his voice filled with excitement. "The Sunken Ruins lie just beyond that ridge. We should prepare ourselves for the dive."

Elara nodded, her resolve firm. "Thank you, Orin. Let's find a safe place to rest and gather our strength before we dive into the depths."

They found a small cove sheltered by rocky cliffs, where they set up a makeshift camp. Elara took the opportunity to rest and prepare, reviewing the map Maelis had given her and making sure her gear was in order. She knew that the journey into the Sunken Ruins would be unlike anything she had faced before, and she needed to be ready for whatever challenges lay ahead.

The Dive Begins

THE NEXT MORNING, AS the sun rose over the horizon, Elara and Orin stood at the water's edge, gazing out at the vast expanse of the ocean. The water was clear and inviting, but Elara knew that it held many dangers beneath its surface.

With a deep breath, she donned her diving gear, which included a special breathing apparatus given to her by Maelis. The device allowed her to breathe underwater for extended periods, a crucial tool for exploring the Sunken Ruins. Orin perched on a nearby rock, his eyes filled with concern and encouragement.

"Be careful, Elara," Orin said. "The sea is both beautiful and treacherous. Trust your instincts and stay focused. I will keep watch from above and guide you as best I can."

Elara nodded, her heart pounding with anticipation. "Thank you, Orin. I'll be back with the Golden Seaweed."

With that, Elara waded into the water, the cool waves lapping at her legs. She took a deep breath and dove beneath the surface, the world above disappearing in a burst of bubbles.

Entering the Sunken Ruins

AS ELARA DESCENDED into the depths, the sunlight filtering through the water created a mesmerizing dance of light and shadow. The ocean was alive with vibrant marine life, schools of fish darting around her, and colorful corals swaying in the gentle currents. The beauty of the underwater world filled her with a sense of wonder, but she remained focused on her mission.

Following the map and the guidance of the enchanted shell, Elara swam deeper, the pressure increasing as she ventured further into the ocean. The water grew colder and darker, and the sense of isolation intensified. She knew she was nearing the Sunken Ruins, and her heart quickened with anticipation.

Finally, after what felt like an eternity, the ruins came into view. The Sunken Ruins were a sprawling underwater city, with ancient stone structures covered in algae and coral. The architecture was both grand and eerie, a testament to a long-lost civilization that had once thrived beneath the waves.

Elara swam through the labyrinthine streets of the ruins, her eyes scanning the surroundings for any sign of the Golden Seaweed. The ruins were filled with the remnants of a bygone era—statues, temples, and intricate carvings that hinted at the city's former glory.

Battling Sea Creatures

AS ELARA EXPLORED THE ruins, she encountered a variety of sea creatures, some curious and others hostile. Schools of fish swam around her, their shimmering scales creating a kaleidoscope of colors. She saw graceful manta rays gliding through the water and even caught a glimpse of a majestic sea turtle.

But not all the creatures were friendly. As she ventured deeper into the ruins, she came face to face with a giant eel, its eyes glowing with a predatory gleam. The eel lunged at her, its powerful jaws snapping dangerously close. Elara dodged to the side, her heart racing as she struggled to outmaneuver the creature.

Using her agility and quick thinking, Elara grabbed a piece of broken coral and used it to fend off the eel. The creature hissed in frustration, but eventually retreated into the shadows, leaving Elara to continue her journey.

The encounter left her shaken but more determined than ever. She knew that the dangers of the Sunken Ruins were real, but she was ready to face them head-on. With renewed resolve, she pressed on, guided by the map and the enchanted shell.

Discovering Ancient Secrets

AS ELARA SWAM THROUGH the ruins, she uncovered several ancient secrets that hinted at the history and culture of the underwater city. She found murals depicting scenes of everyday life, rituals, and ceremonies, all intricately carved into the stone walls. The murals told a story of a civilization that had once thrived beneath the waves, its people living in harmony with the ocean.

In one of the larger chambers, Elara discovered a massive statue of a sea goddess, her arms outstretched in a gesture of blessing. The statue was covered in glowing seaweed, its light casting an ethereal glow over the chamber. Elara felt a sense of reverence and awe as she gazed at the statue, feeling a deep connection to the ancient civilization.

She also found several artifacts, including ornate jewelry, pottery, and weapons. Each item was a testament to the skill and craftsmanship of the people who had once inhabited the ruins. Elara carefully collected a few of the artifacts, hoping to bring them back to the surface as a way to honor the memory of the lost civilization.

Finding the Golden Seaweed

AFTER HOURS OF SEARCHING, Elara finally found what she had been looking for—the Golden Seaweed. It grew in a secluded garden at the heart of the ruins, its golden fronds swaying gently in the currents. The seaweed glowed with an otherworldly light, and Elara knew that it was the third ingredient needed to break Seraphina's curse.

She carefully approached the garden, her heart pounding with excitement. As she reached out to collect the seaweed, she felt a sense of triumph and relief. The journey had been long and difficult, but she had succeeded in finding the Golden Seaweed.

Just as she was about to collect the seaweed, a shadow passed over her. Elara looked up to see a massive sea serpent coiling through the water, its scales shimmering with an iridescent glow. The serpent's eyes locked onto her, and it let out a low, rumbling growl.

Elara knew that she was in for a battle. She braced herself, gripping her knife tightly as the serpent lunged at her. The creature was fast and powerful, but Elara was determined to protect the Golden Seaweed and complete her mission.

The Battle with the Sea Serpent

THE SEA SERPENT'S ATTACK was swift and relentless. It lunged at Elara with its massive jaws, its teeth glinting in the dim light. Elara dodged to the side, narrowly avoiding the creature's bite. She swung her knife, aiming for the serpent's vulnerable underbelly, but the creature's scales were tough and resistant.

The serpent thrashed in the water, creating powerful currents that threatened to sweep Elara away. She fought to maintain her balance, using her agility and quick reflexes to dodge the serpent's attacks. She knew that she needed to find a way to outsmart the creature and exploit its weaknesses.

As the battle raged on, Elara noticed that the serpent's eyes were its most vulnerable point. She waited for the right moment, then lunged forward, plunging her knife into one of the serpent's eyes. The creature let out a deafening roar of pain, thrashing wildly as it tried to dislodge her.

Elara held on tightly, her determination unwavering. She twisted the knife, driving it deeper into the serpent's eye. The creature's movements grew more frantic, but Elara refused to let go. Finally, with a final, powerful thrust, she drove the knife deep into the serpent's brain, killing it instantly.

The serpent's body went limp, sinking slowly to the ocean floor. Elara pulled the knife free, her heart pounding with adrenaline and relief. She had defeated the sea serpent and protected the Golden Seaweed.

Collecting the Golden Seaweed

WITH THE SEA SERPENT defeated, Elara turned her attention back to the Golden Seaweed. She carefully collected several fronds, placing them in a special container designed to preserve their magical properties. The seaweed glowed softly, its light filling her with a sense of hope and accomplishment.

Elara knew that the journey was far from over, but she felt a renewed sense of determination. She had faced many challenges and overcome great dangers, and she was ready to continue her quest to break Seraphina's curse.

Uncovering More Secrets

AS ELARA PREPARED TO leave the Sunken Ruins, she decided to explore a few more chambers in the hope of uncovering additional secrets and treasures. She swam through the labyrinthine streets, her eyes scanning the surroundings for any signs of hidden passageways or chambers.

In one of the deeper chambers, she discovered a hidden doorway concealed behind a thick curtain of seaweed. She pushed the seaweed aside and swam through the doorway, entering a large, domed chamber filled with intricate carvings and murals.

The chamber was filled with artifacts and treasures, including ornate jewelry, pottery, and weapons. Elara carefully examined each item, marveling at the skill and craftsmanship of the ancient civilization. She collected a few of the artifacts, hoping to bring them back to the surface as a way to honor the memory of the lost city.

As she explored the chamber, Elara found a large, intricately carved chest at the center of the room. The chest was covered in glowing runes, and Elara could feel a powerful energy emanating from it. She carefully opened the chest, revealing a collection of ancient scrolls and manuscripts.

The scrolls were written in a language Elara couldn't understand, but she knew that they contained valuable knowledge and secrets. She carefully collected the scrolls, hoping to find a way to translate them once she returned to the surface.

Return to the Surface

WITH THE GOLDEN SEAWEED and the ancient scrolls safely secured, Elara began her journey back to the surface. The ascent was long and challenging, but she felt a sense of triumph and accomplishment as she swam through the ruins and back toward the light.

As she emerged from the depths, the sunlight filtered through the water, creating a dazzling display of colors. Elara took a deep breath of fresh air, feeling the warmth of the sun on her face. She had succeeded in retrieving the Golden Seaweed and uncovering valuable secrets from the Sunken Ruins.

Orin flew down to meet her, his eyes filled with pride and relief. "You did it, Elara," he said. "You found the Golden Seaweed and uncovered the secrets of the ruins. I knew you could do it."

Elara smiled, feeling a deep sense of satisfaction. "Thank you, Orin. I couldn't have done it without your guidance and support."

Returning to Seraphina

WITH THE GOLDEN SEAWEED and the ancient scrolls in hand, Elara and Orin began their journey back to the hidden cove. The journey was filled with a sense of accomplishment and anticipation, as Elara looked forward to sharing her success with Seraphina.

As they approached the cove, Elara saw Seraphina waiting for her, a look of hopeful anticipation in her eyes. Elara knelt at the water's edge and held out the container of Golden Seaweed.

"I have the seaweed, Seraphina," she said, her voice filled with pride. "What do we do next?"

Seraphina's eyes sparkled with gratitude and relief. "Thank you, Elara. The third ingredient is ours. Now we must gather the Shadow Berries from the Island of Shadows. It will be a difficult journey, but I have faith in you."

Elara nodded, feeling a renewed sense of determination. "I will head to the island at once. We will break this curse, Seraphina. I promise."

Seraphina smiled, her eyes shining with hope. "I know you will, Elara. You are a true friend and a brave soul. The sea is with you, always."

With those words, Elara felt a surge of confidence and purpose. She tucked the container of Golden Seaweed safely into her satchel and turned to leave the cove, ready to face the next challenge on her quest.

Journey to the Island of Shadows

THE JOURNEY TO THE Island of Shadows took Elara and Orin through dense forests, across rushing rivers, and over rugged terrain. The landscape was ever-changing, filled with both beauty and danger. Despite the challenges, Elara pressed on, driven by her determination to retrieve the Shadow Berries and break Seraphina's curse.

As they traveled, Elara and Orin encountered various mythical creatures and faced numerous challenges. Each obstacle tested their resolve and strengthened their bond, forging a deep sense of trust and friendship between them.

Finally, after many days of travel, they reached the coast where the Island of Shadows lay hidden beyond the horizon. The ocean stretched out before them, vast and mysterious, its surface glinting in the sunlight.

Elara stood at the water's edge, her heart filled with anticipation and determination. The journey ahead would be treacherous, but she was ready to face whatever challenges came her way.

With Orin by her side and the guidance of the enchanted shell, Elara prepared to sail to the Island of Shadows and retrieve the Shadow Berries. The echoes of her success in the Sunken Ruins resonated in her heart, a constant reminder of the bond she shared with Seraphina and the destiny that awaited them both.

And so, with the third ingredient secured and the promise of more adventures to come, Elara set off toward the Island of Shadows, her heart filled with hope and her spirit unyielding. The mysterious voice of Seraphina echoed in her mind, a constant reminder of the bond they shared and the destiny that awaited them both.

Chapter 8: The Island of Shadows

The Journey Begins

The sun was just beginning to rise, casting a golden glow over the ocean as Elara prepared to set sail for the Island of Shadows. The journey to retrieve the Shadow Berries, the final ingredient needed to break Seraphina's curse, promised to be the most challenging yet. The Island of Shadows was shrouded in mystery and legend, a place where light and darkness intertwined and where one's deepest fears were said to come to life.

Elara stood at the water's edge, her heart pounding with anticipation. She had faced many challenges on her quest, each one strengthening her resolve and deepening her connection to the sea and the magical world it concealed. With Orin perched on her shoulder, his golden eyes filled with wisdom and encouragement, she felt ready to confront whatever lay ahead.

"The Island of Shadows is a place of great power," Orin said, his voice calm but serious. "It is said that those who venture there must confront their inner darkness and find balance between light and shadow. You will need all your courage and determination to succeed."

Elara nodded, her resolve firm. "I understand, Orin. I'm ready to face whatever challenges come my way. We need those Shadow Berries to free Seraphina, and I won't let anything stop us."

With that, Elara boarded a small, sturdy boat she had prepared for the journey. The boat was equipped with supplies for the voyage, including food, water, and the enchanted shell that had guided her on her quest. As she set sail, the waves gently lapped against the hull, carrying her toward the distant island.

The Voyage

THE JOURNEY ACROSS the ocean was long and arduous, with the boat navigating through both calm seas and turbulent storms. Elara remained vigilant, her eyes scanning the horizon for any sign of the Island of Shadows. The enchanted shell glowed softly, providing a sense of direction and comfort.

Days turned into nights as Elara sailed onward, her determination unwavering. She faced various challenges along the way, from fierce storms that threatened to capsize the boat to encounters with curious sea creatures. Each obstacle tested her resolve, but she pressed on, driven by her commitment to free Seraphina.

One night, as the stars twinkled above and the sea was calm, Elara sat at the bow of the boat, lost in thought. Orin flew down to perch beside her, his presence a constant source of comfort and guidance.

"We're getting closer, Elara," Orin said softly. "I can feel it. The Island of Shadows is near."

Elara nodded, her gaze fixed on the horizon. "Thank you, Orin. I couldn't have come this far without you."

As dawn broke, casting a warm glow over the ocean, Elara saw a dark shape emerging from the mist. The Island of Shadows loomed ahead, its rugged cliffs and dense forests shrouded in an eerie, otherworldly light. The island seemed to pulse with a strange energy, both inviting and foreboding.

Taking a deep breath, Elara steered the boat toward the island, her heart pounding with anticipation and resolve. She knew that the journey ahead would be filled with challenges, but she was ready to face them head-on.

Arrival at the Island of Shadows

THE BOAT GENTLY BUMPED against the shore as Elara arrived at the Island of Shadows. She secured the boat and stepped onto the beach, her senses heightened by the island's mysterious energy. The air was thick with a palpable tension, and the sounds of the ocean seemed muted, as if the island absorbed all noise.

The beach was lined with dark, jagged rocks, and the dense forest beyond beckoned with an eerie allure. The shadows seemed to move and shift, creating an ever-changing landscape that was both beautiful and unsettling.

Orin flew up to a nearby tree branch, his eyes scanning the surroundings. "The Shadow Berries are said to grow deep within the heart of the island," he said. "But be cautious, Elara. The island will test you in ways you cannot yet imagine. You must confront your own inner darkness and find balance between light and shadow."

Elara nodded, her resolve unwavering. "I'm ready, Orin. Let's find those berries and free Seraphina."

With Orin guiding her from above, Elara began her journey into the heart of the island. The forest was dense and overgrown, with twisted trees and thick underbrush that made progress slow and difficult. The shadows seemed to cling to her, and the air was filled with an oppressive silence that weighed heavily on her mind.

As she ventured deeper into the forest, Elara felt a growing sense of unease. The shadows seemed to whisper and move, creating an ever-present sense of being watched. She reminded herself of Seraphina's plight and her commitment to freeing the mermaid, using her determination to push through her fear.

Confronting Inner Darkness

AS ELARA NAVIGATED the dense forest, she came upon a clearing bathed in an eerie, dim light. The clearing was surrounded by ancient trees, their gnarled branches intertwining to form a natural barrier. In the center of the clearing stood a large, reflective pool of water, its surface perfectly still.

Elara approached the pool cautiously, her reflection staring back at her from the dark, mirrored surface. As she gazed into the water, she felt a strange pull, as if the pool were drawing her in. She knelt at the edge, peering deeper into the reflection.

Suddenly, the water rippled, and Elara's reflection began to change. The image distorted, showing a twisted version of herself, filled with anger, fear, and doubt. The reflection spoke, its voice a haunting echo of her own.

"Who are you, Elara?" the reflection hissed. "You think you can save Seraphina? You are weak, filled with fear and doubt. You will fail."

Elara recoiled, her heart pounding with fear. The reflection's words cut deep, echoing her own insecurities and fears. She had faced many challenges on her quest, but this was different. This was a confrontation with her own inner darkness.

Taking a deep breath, Elara forced herself to stand tall. "I am Elara," she said firmly. "I have faced many challenges and overcome great obstacles. I will not be defeated by my own fears and doubts."

The reflection laughed, its twisted features contorting with mockery. "You are nothing, Elara. Just a girl with dreams too big for her. You will never succeed."

Elara's resolve hardened. "I may be afraid, but I am not weak. I have the strength to overcome my fears and find the light within the darkness. I will succeed, not just for Seraphina, but for myself."

With those words, Elara reached out and touched the surface of the pool. The water rippled, and the reflection shattered, dissolving into nothingness. The oppressive silence lifted, and the shadows around her seemed to retreat.

Elara felt a sense of relief and triumph. She had confronted her inner darkness and emerged stronger. The journey ahead would still be challenging, but she knew she had the strength to face it.

The Path to the Heart of the Island

WITH A RENEWED SENSE of determination, Elara continued her journey into the heart of the island. The forest seemed less daunting now, the shadows less oppressive. She felt a deep connection to the island, as if it had accepted her as a worthy ally.

Orin flew down to perch on her shoulder, his eyes filled with pride. "You did well, Elara," he said. "The island's tests are not easy, but you faced them with courage and grace."

Elara smiled, feeling a deep sense of connection to her friend. "Thank you, Orin. I couldn't have done it without you."

As they ventured deeper into the forest, Elara noticed that the landscape began to change. The trees grew taller and more majestic, their branches forming intricate patterns against the sky. The ground was covered in soft moss and delicate wildflowers, and the air was filled with the sweet scent of blooming plants.

They came upon a narrow path that led to a hidden grove, bathed in a soft, ethereal light. The grove was filled with shimmering, silver leaves and glowing flowers, creating a magical, otherworldly atmosphere.

In the center of the grove stood a large, ancient tree, its branches heavy with clusters of dark, glowing berries. Elara knew instinctively that these were the Shadow Berries she sought.

The Guardian of the Berries

AS ELARA APPROACHED the ancient tree, a figure emerged from the shadows. It was a tall, ethereal being with flowing robes and eyes that glowed with an inner light. The guardian radiated an aura of power and wisdom, and Elara felt a mixture of fear and respect as she approached.

"Welcome, Elara," the guardian said, its voice a harmonious blend of many tones. "You have come for the Shadow Berries, but first, you must prove yourself worthy. The balance between light and shadow is delicate, and only those who understand this balance may take the berries."

Elara nodded, her resolve firm. "I am ready to face any challenge. I seek the Shadow Berries to break a curse and free Seraphina."

The guardian's eyes softened, and it nodded in approval. "Very well. You must pass the Trial of Balance. You will be tested on your understanding of light and shadow, and your ability to find harmony between them."

With a graceful gesture, the guardian beckoned Elara forward. The ground beneath her feet shifted, and she found herself standing on a narrow, suspended bridge that stretched across a deep chasm. The bridge swayed gently, and the chasm below was shrouded in darkness.

The Trial of Balance

ELARA TOOK A DEEP BREATH, focusing on her inner strength and determination. She stepped onto the bridge, feeling the delicate balance between light and shadow. The bridge swayed gently with each step, and Elara knew that she needed to maintain her composure and focus to succeed.

As she walked, the shadows around her seemed to shift and move, creating illusions and distractions. She saw visions of her past, moments of fear and doubt that threatened to unbalance her. But Elara remained steadfast, using her understanding of light and shadow to find harmony within herself.

Halfway across the bridge, the air grew colder, and the shadows deepened. Elara felt a sense of foreboding, but she pressed on, her resolve unwavering. She knew that the trial was not just about physical balance, but also about inner harmony.

With each step, Elara focused on her breath, finding a rhythm that matched the sway of the bridge. She allowed herself to acknowledge her fears and doubts, but did not let them control her. Instead, she found a sense of peace within the balance of light and shadow.

Finally, after what felt like an eternity, Elara reached the other side of the bridge. The guardian awaited her, its eyes filled with approval.

"You have passed the Trial of Balance," the guardian said. "You have shown great understanding and harmony. The Shadow Berries are yours to take."

Collecting the Shadow Berries

WITH THE GUARDIAN'S approval, Elara approached the ancient tree. She carefully collected several clusters of the glowing berries, placing them in a special container designed to preserve their magical properties. The berries pulsed with a soft, ethereal light, and Elara knew that they were the final ingredient needed to break Seraphina's curse.

As she finished collecting the berries, Elara felt a deep sense of accomplishment and relief. The journey had been long and difficult, but she had succeeded in finding the Shadow Berries.

The guardian stepped forward, its eyes filled with wisdom. "You have done well, Elara. The balance between light and shadow is a delicate one, and you have shown great understanding and strength. May these berries aid you in your quest."

Elara bowed her head in gratitude. "Thank you. I will use them to break Seraphina's curse and restore harmony."

With the Shadow Berries safely secured, Elara and Orin began their journey back to the shore. The forest seemed less daunting now, its shadows more welcoming. Elara felt a deep connection to the island, as if it had become a part of her.

Return to Seraphina

THE JOURNEY BACK TO the hidden cove was filled with a sense of accomplishment and anticipation. Elara had faced her inner darkness and found balance within herself. She had retrieved the final ingredient needed to break Seraphina's curse.

As they approached the cove, Elara saw Seraphina waiting for her, a look of hopeful anticipation in her eyes. Elara knelt at the water's edge and held out the container of Shadow Berries.

"I have the berries, Seraphina," she said, her voice filled with pride. "We have all the ingredients. What do we do next?"

Seraphina's eyes sparkled with gratitude and relief. "Thank you, Elara. You have done it. Now we must prepare the potion to break the curse. With the Moonflower petals, the Echoing Crystals, the Golden Seaweed, and the Shadow Berries, we can finally set me free."

Elara nodded, feeling a renewed sense of determination. "Let's do it. I'm ready to help you break the curse."

Preparing the Potion

WITH ALL THE INGREDIENTS gathered, Elara and Seraphina set to work preparing the potion. Seraphina guided Elara through the intricate process, explaining each step and the significance of the ingredients. The enchanted shell glowed softly, providing a sense of direction and comfort.

Elara carefully combined the Moonflower petals, the Echoing Crystals, the Golden Seaweed, and the Shadow Berries, mixing them in a special container designed to preserve their magical properties. The potion glowed with an ethereal light, its energy resonating with the power of the ingredients.

As they worked, Elara felt a deep connection to the magic and the ancient wisdom that had guided her on her quest. She knew that she was part of something greater, a legacy of harmony and balance that stretched back through the ages.

Finally, the potion was complete. Seraphina held the container in her hands, her eyes filled with hope and determination.

"Thank you, Elara," Seraphina said softly. "With this potion, we can break the curse and restore balance. You have shown great courage and strength, and I am forever grateful."

Elara smiled, feeling a deep sense of accomplishment and pride. "It has been an honor to help you, Seraphina. Let's break this curse and set you free."

Breaking the Curse

WITH THE POTION IN hand, Seraphina and Elara performed a series of ancient rituals to break the curse. The rituals were complex and precise, requiring both focus and intent. Seraphina chanted ancient incantations, her voice filled with power and grace, while Elara assisted with the preparation and application of the potion.

As the rituals progressed, the air around them seemed to shimmer with magical energy. The potion glowed brighter, its light pulsing in rhythm with Seraphina's chants. Elara felt a deep sense of connection to the magic and the ancient wisdom that had guided her on her quest.

Finally, with a final, powerful incantation, Seraphina poured the potion over herself. The potion glowed with a blinding light, and the air was filled with a resonant hum that seemed to vibrate through the very fabric of reality.

Elara watched in awe as the potion's magic took effect. The curse that had bound Seraphina for so long began to dissolve, its dark tendrils unraveling and dissipating into the air. Seraphina's form glowed with a radiant light, her eyes filled with joy and relief.

As the light faded, Seraphina stood before Elara, her form free of the curse. The enchantment that had bound her to the cove was broken, and she was once again a free and powerful guardian of the sea.

"Thank you, Elara," Seraphina said, her voice filled with emotion. "You have set me free. I am forever grateful for your courage and determination."

Elara felt a deep sense of fulfillment and pride. "It has been an honor to help you, Seraphina. I am glad to have been a part of your journey."

Celebrating Victory

WITH THE CURSE BROKEN and Seraphina free, Elara and Orin celebrated their victory. They returned to the village of Marinia, where they were greeted with joy and celebration. The villagers had heard of Elara's quest and were filled with admiration for her bravery and determination.

A grand feast was held in Elara's honor, with food, music, and dancing. The villagers celebrated not only Elara's victory but also the restoration of harmony and balance to the sea. Elara felt a deep sense of connection to her community and to the magical world she had discovered.

As the celebration continued, Elara found a quiet moment to reflect on her journey. She had faced many challenges, confronted her inner darkness, and found balance within herself. She had formed deep connections with Seraphina and Orin, and had uncovered ancient secrets and wisdom.

Elara knew that her journey was far from over. There were still many mysteries to explore and many challenges to face. But she felt a deep sense of confidence and determination, knowing that she had the strength and courage to overcome whatever lay ahead.

A New Beginning

AS THE SUN SET OVER the ocean, casting a golden glow over the village, Elara stood at the water's edge, gazing out at the horizon. The sea was calm and inviting, filled with the promise of new adventures and discoveries.

Seraphina emerged from the water, her eyes filled with gratitude and determination. "Thank you, Elara," she said softly. "You have set me free and restored balance to the sea. I am forever grateful."

Elara smiled, feeling a deep sense of fulfillment. "It has been an honor to help you, Seraphina. I look forward to our future adventures together."

Orin flew down to perch on Elara's shoulder, his golden eyes filled with wisdom and encouragement. "The journey has been long and challenging, but you have shown great courage and strength. I am proud to call you my friend."

Elara felt a deep sense of connection to her friends and to the magical world she had discovered. She knew that there were still many mysteries to explore and many challenges to face, but she was ready for whatever lay ahead.

And so, with the promise of new adventures and the support of her friends, Elara set off on a new journey, her heart filled with hope and her spirit unyielding. The echoes of her success resonated in her heart, a constant reminder of the bond she shared with Seraphina and the destiny that awaited them both.

Chapter 9: The Gathering Storm

Returning to the Cove

With the Shadow Berries safely secured, Elara felt a profound sense of accomplishment and relief. She had gathered all the ingredients needed to break Seraphina's curse, and now, the final step of their journey was within reach. As she and Orin made their way back to the hidden cove, Elara's heart was filled with hope and determination.

The journey back to the cove took several days. The landscape seemed more vibrant and welcoming than before, as if the world itself acknowledged Elara's achievements. Orin, ever vigilant, flew above her, keeping watch for any signs of danger.

As they neared the cove, Elara could sense a change in the air. The sky grew darker, and the wind picked up, whipping through the trees with increasing intensity. Elara knew that Morgana, the sea witch who had cursed Seraphina, was aware of their progress and would stop at nothing to thwart them.

"We must hurry, Orin," Elara said, her voice resolute. "Morgana will not let us break the curse without a fight."

Orin nodded, his golden eyes filled with determination. "Let's move quickly, Elara. We must reach Seraphina before the storm."

The Storm Approaches

AS THEY APPROACHED the cove, the sky darkened further, and the wind grew stronger. Thunder rumbled in the distance, and lightning flashed across the sky. Elara could feel the malevolent presence of Morgana in the storm, her dark magic swirling through the air.

When they finally reached the cove, Seraphina was waiting for them, her eyes filled with a mixture of hope and concern. The waves crashed against the shore with increasing ferocity, and the air was thick with the promise of a tempest.

"Elara, you've returned," Seraphina said, her voice filled with relief. "But we must act quickly. Morgana knows what we are trying to do, and she will do everything in her power to stop us."

Elara nodded, her resolve firm. "We have all the ingredients. Let's break this curse once and for all."

Preparing the Potion

WITH THE STORM RAPIDLY approaching, Elara and Seraphina set to work preparing the potion to break the curse. The enchanted shell glowed softly, providing a sense of direction and comfort. Seraphina guided Elara through the intricate process, explaining each step and the significance of the ingredients.

Elara carefully combined the Moonflower petals, the Echoing Crystals, the Golden Seaweed, and the Shadow Berries, mixing them in a special container designed to preserve their magical properties. The potion glowed with an ethereal light, its energy resonating with the power of the ingredients.

As they worked, the storm grew more intense. The wind howled, and the waves crashed against the shore with increasing ferocity. Thunder boomed overhead, and lightning lit up the sky, casting eerie shadows across the cove.

"We must hurry," Seraphina said, her voice filled with urgency. "Morgana's storm is growing stronger. We need to complete the potion and perform the ritual before it's too late."

Elara nodded, her hands steady as she continued to mix the potion. Despite the chaos around them, she felt a deep sense of focus and determination. She knew that this was their only chance to break the curse and set Seraphina free.

The Ritual Begins

WITH THE POTION COMPLETE, Seraphina and Elara moved to the center of the cove. The wind whipped around them, and the waves crashed violently against the shore. Morgana's presence was palpable, her dark magic swirling through the storm.

Seraphina held the container of potion in her hands, her eyes filled with determination. "Thank you, Elara," she said softly. "You have shown great courage and strength. Now, we must perform the ritual to break the curse."

Elara nodded, her resolve unwavering. "Let's do it. I'm ready."

Seraphina began to chant ancient incantations, her voice filled with power and grace. The potion glowed brighter, its light pulsing in rhythm with her chants. Elara stood by her side, assisting with the ritual and providing support.

As the ritual progressed, the air around them seemed to shimmer with magical energy. The potion's light intensified, casting a radiant glow over the cove. Elara felt a deep connection to the magic and the ancient wisdom that had guided her on her quest.

Finally, with a final, powerful incantation, Seraphina poured the potion over herself. The potion glowed with a blinding light, and the air was filled with a resonant hum that seemed to vibrate through the very fabric of reality.

Elara watched in awe as the potion's magic took effect. The curse that had bound Seraphina for so long began to dissolve, its dark tendrils unraveling and dissipating into the air. Seraphina's form glowed with a radiant light, her eyes filled with joy and relief.

But just as the curse began to break, a powerful gust of wind tore through the cove, nearly knocking Elara off her feet. Morgana's storm had reached its peak, and the sea witch's dark magic surged through the air, threatening to undo their efforts.

The Final Confrontation

A FIGURE EMERGED FROM the storm, her presence dark and malevolent. Morgana, the sea witch, had arrived. Her eyes glowed with a sinister light, and her form was shrouded in swirling shadows. She raised her hands, and the storm intensified, lightning crackling around her.

"You think you can break my curse?" Morgana hissed, her voice filled with venom. "You are nothing but a foolish girl and a cursed mermaid. I will not let you succeed."

Elara stepped forward, her heart pounding with fear and determination. "We will break the curse, Morgana," she said, her voice steady. "Your reign of darkness ends here."

Morgana laughed, a chilling sound that echoed through the storm. "You are brave, but foolish. You cannot defeat me."

With a wave of her hand, Morgana summoned a powerful wave that crashed toward Elara and Seraphina. Elara braced herself, using her magic to create a barrier that deflected the wave. The force of the impact nearly knocked her off her feet, but she stood firm.

Seraphina joined Elara, her own magic glowing with a radiant light. Together, they faced Morgana, their combined strength and determination creating a powerful force of light.

"You cannot stop us, Morgana," Seraphina said, her voice filled with resolve. "We will break the curse and restore balance to the sea."

Morgana's eyes narrowed, and she unleashed a torrent of dark magic, sending bolts of energy toward Elara and Seraphina. Elara raised her hands, using her magic to deflect the attacks. The air crackled with energy as the forces of light and darkness clashed.

The Battle Rages On

THE BATTLE RAGED ON, the storm growing ever more intense. Lightning flashed across the sky, and thunder boomed, shaking the very ground beneath their feet. The wind howled, and the waves crashed with a fury that matched the intensity of the battle.

Elara and Seraphina fought with all their strength, their combined magic creating a radiant barrier of light that pushed back against Morgana's darkness. But Morgana was powerful, her dark magic relentless and unyielding.

As the battle continued, Elara felt her strength waning. The effort of maintaining the barrier and deflecting Morgana's attacks was taking its toll. She glanced at Seraphina, who was also struggling to keep up the fight.

"We can't give up," Elara said, her voice filled with determination. "We have to break the curse."

Seraphina nodded, her eyes filled with resolve. "We must hold on. We can do this, Elara."

With renewed determination, Elara and Seraphina focused their magic, channeling their combined strength into a powerful surge of light. The barrier around them glowed brighter, pushing back against Morgana's dark magic.

Morgana let out a furious scream, her eyes blazing with anger. "You will not defeat me!" she hissed, summoning all her power for a final, devastating attack.

A massive bolt of dark energy surged toward Elara and Seraphina, its power overwhelming. Elara braced herself, using every ounce of her strength to deflect the attack. The impact was immense, the force of it nearly knocking her off her feet.

But as the dust settled, Elara realized that their barrier had held. The dark energy dissipated, leaving Morgana standing before them, her power spent and her form weakened.

The Tide Turns

WITH MORGANA'S POWER weakened, Elara and Seraphina saw their chance. They channeled their magic into a final, powerful surge of light, directing it toward the sea witch. The radiant energy enveloped Morgana, dispelling the darkness that surrounded her.

Morgana let out a final, anguished scream as the light overcame her. The shadows around her dissipated, and her form dissolved into the air, leaving nothing but a faint, lingering mist.

The storm began to subside, the wind dying down and the waves calming. The dark clouds that had covered the sky began to part, revealing the first rays of sunlight breaking through.

Elara and Seraphina stood together, their hands still glowing with the remnants of their magic. The air was filled with a sense of peace and relief, the oppressive darkness lifted.

"We did it," Elara said softly, her voice filled with awe. "We broke the curse."

Seraphina smiled, her eyes shining with gratitude. "Yes, Elara. Thanks to you, we have restored balance to the sea."

The Aftermath

WITH THE CURSE BROKEN and Morgana defeated, Elara and Seraphina returned to the village of Marinia. The villagers greeted them with joy and celebration, their hearts filled with gratitude and admiration for Elara's bravery and determination.

A grand feast was held in Elara's honor, with food, music, and dancing. The villagers celebrated not only Elara's victory but also the restoration of harmony and balance to the sea. Elara felt a deep sense of connection to her community and to the magical world she had discovered.

As the celebration continued, Elara found a quiet moment to reflect on her journey. She had faced many challenges, confronted her inner darkness, and found balance within herself. She had formed deep connections with Seraphina and Orin, and had uncovered ancient secrets and wisdom.

Elara knew that her journey was far from over. There were still many mysteries to explore and many challenges to face. But she felt a deep sense of confidence and determination, knowing that she had the strength and courage to overcome whatever lay ahead.

A New Dawn

AS THE SUN ROSE OVER the ocean, casting a golden glow over the village, Elara stood at the water's edge, gazing out at the horizon. The sea was calm and inviting, filled with the promise of new adventures and discoveries.

Seraphina emerged from the water, her eyes filled with gratitude and determination. "Thank you, Elara," she said softly. "You have set me free and restored balance to the sea. I am forever grateful."

Elara smiled, feeling a deep sense of fulfillment. "It has been an honor to help you, Seraphina. I look forward to our future adventures together."

Orin flew down to perch on Elara's shoulder, his golden eyes filled with wisdom and encouragement. "The journey has been long and challenging, but you have shown great courage and strength. I am proud to call you my friend."

Elara felt a deep sense of connection to her friends and to the magical world she had discovered. She knew that there were still many mysteries to explore and many challenges to face, but she was ready for whatever lay ahead.

And so, with the promise of new adventures and the support of her friends, Elara set off on a new journey, her heart filled with hope and her spirit unyielding. The echoes of her success resonated in her heart, a constant reminder of the bond she shared with Seraphina and the destiny that awaited them both.

The storm had passed, and a new dawn had begun. Elara's journey was far from over, but she was ready to face whatever lay ahead, knowing that she had the strength and courage to overcome any obstacle. The sea, with all its magic and mystery, awaited her, and she was ready to embrace her destiny.

Chapter 10: The Battle at Sea

The Calm Before the Storm

The days following the breaking of Seraphina's curse were filled with joy and celebration. The village of Marinia buzzed with excitement as the news of Elara's bravery spread. The sea, once dark and turbulent under Morgana's influence, now shimmered with a serene beauty. Elara felt a profound sense of peace, but also a lingering unease. She knew that Morgana was still out there, her malevolent presence a dark cloud over their newfound peace.

Elara stood at the water's edge, gazing out at the horizon. The sun was setting, casting a golden glow over the ocean. Seraphina emerged from the water, her eyes filled with gratitude and determination.

"Elara, we have achieved much, but Morgana's threat still looms," Seraphina said, her voice filled with concern. "She will not rest until she regains her power and control over the sea."

Elara nodded, her resolve firm. "We must be prepared for whatever she plans next. The villagers need to be warned and ready to defend themselves."

As the evening deepened, Elara and Seraphina gathered the villagers in the town square. Elara stood before them, her heart pounding with the weight of responsibility. She could see the trust and admiration in their eyes, and she knew that they would stand with her.

"Friends, we have faced great challenges and emerged victorious," Elara began, her voice steady. "But our fight is not over. Morgana is still a threat, and we must be ready to defend our village and our sea."

The villagers murmured in agreement, their faces filled with determination. Finn, Elara's father, stepped forward, his eyes shining with pride and resolve.

"We will stand with you, Elara," Finn said firmly. "Whatever comes, we will face it together."

Preparing for Battle

THE DAYS THAT FOLLOWED were filled with preparation and training. Elara, Seraphina, and the villagers worked tirelessly to fortify the village and ready themselves for the impending battle. Weapons were sharpened, defenses were strengthened, and strategies were devised.

Elara trained with the villagers, teaching them the skills she had learned on her journey. She showed them how to fight with courage and determination, and how to use the magic of the sea to their advantage. Seraphina used her own magic to enhance their defenses, creating barriers and wards to protect the village.

As they prepared, Elara felt a deep sense of unity and purpose. The villagers were no longer fearful; they were ready to fight for their home and their freedom. Elara knew that the battle ahead would be fierce, but she also knew that they had the strength and courage to face it.

The Storm Breaks

ON THE MORNING OF THE battle, the sky was filled with dark, swirling clouds. The air was thick with tension, and the sea churned with a restless energy. Elara stood at the shore, her heart pounding with anticipation. She could feel Morgana's presence, a dark force gathering on the horizon.

Seraphina emerged from the water, her eyes filled with determination. "It is time, Elara. Morgana is coming."

Elara nodded, her resolve firm. "Let's face her together."

As the storm approached, the villagers gathered at the shore, their faces filled with a mixture of fear and determination. Finn stood beside Elara, his hand resting on her shoulder.

"We are with you, Elara," Finn said, his voice steady. "We will fight together."

The first wave of Morgana's attack came in the form of a powerful storm. The wind howled, and the waves crashed violently against the shore. Lightning flashed across the sky, illuminating the dark clouds with a blinding light.

Elara raised her hands, using her magic to create a barrier that shielded the village from the worst of the storm. Seraphina joined her, their combined magic creating a powerful force of light that pushed back against the darkness.

The Battle Begins

MORGANA'S FORCES EMERGED from the storm, a legion of dark creatures and twisted sea monsters. The villagers stood ready, their weapons at the ready and their hearts filled with resolve.

The battle began with a fierce clash of steel and magic. Elara and Seraphina led the charge, their combined strength and determination driving them forward. The villagers fought bravely, inspired by Elara's courage and the strength of their unity.

Elara faced off against a massive sea serpent, its eyes glowing with a malevolent light. She dodged its attacks, using her agility and quick reflexes to stay one step ahead. With a powerful surge of magic, she struck the serpent down, her blade slicing through its tough scales.

Seraphina used her magic to create powerful waves that swept away Morgana's forces, her voice filled with the power of the sea. The villagers fought with a fierce determination, their unity and courage giving them the strength to stand against the darkness.

Morgana's Arrival

AS THE BATTLE RAGED on, Morgana herself emerged from the storm, her presence dark and menacing. Her eyes glowed with a sinister light, and her form was shrouded in swirling shadows. She raised her hands, and the storm intensified, lightning crackling around her.

"You think you can defeat me?" Morgana hissed, her voice filled with venom. "You are nothing but a foolish girl and a cursed mermaid. I will not be defeated."

Elara stepped forward, her heart pounding with fear and determination. "We will defeat you, Morgana," she said, her voice steady. "Your reign of darkness ends here."

Morgana laughed, a chilling sound that echoed through the storm. "You are brave, but foolish. You cannot defeat me."

With a wave of her hand, Morgana unleashed a powerful blast of dark magic, sending bolts of energy toward Elara and Seraphina. Elara raised her hands, using her magic to deflect the attacks. The air crackled with energy as the forces of light and darkness clashed.

The Battle Intensifies

THE BATTLE WITH MORGANA was fierce and relentless. The storm raged around them, the wind howling and the waves crashing with a fury that matched the intensity of the fight. Lightning flashed across the sky, illuminating the dark clouds with a blinding light.

Elara and Seraphina fought with all their strength, their combined magic creating a radiant barrier of light that pushed back against Morgana's darkness. But Morgana was powerful, her dark magic relentless and unyielding.

As the battle continued, Elara felt her strength waning. The effort of maintaining the barrier and deflecting Morgana's attacks was taking its toll. She glanced at Seraphina, who was also struggling to keep up the fight.

"We can't give up," Elara said, her voice filled with determination. "We have to defeat her."

Seraphina nodded, her eyes filled with resolve. "We must hold on. We can do this, Elara."

With renewed determination, Elara and Seraphina focused their magic, channeling their combined strength into a powerful surge of light. The barrier around them glowed brighter, pushing back against Morgana's dark magic.

Morgana let out a furious scream, her eyes blazing with anger. "You will not defeat me!" she hissed, summoning all her power for a final, devastating attack.

The Turning Point

A MASSIVE BOLT OF DARK energy surged toward Elara and Seraphina, its power overwhelming. Elara braced herself, using every ounce of her strength to deflect the attack. The impact was immense, the force of it nearly knocking her off her feet.

But as the dust settled, Elara realized that their barrier had held. The dark energy dissipated, leaving Morgana standing before them, her power spent and her form weakened.

With Morgana's power weakened, Elara and Seraphina saw their chance. They channeled their magic into a final, powerful surge of light, directing it toward the sea witch. The radiant energy enveloped Morgana, dispelling the darkness that surrounded her.

Morgana let out a final, anguished scream as the light overcame her. The shadows around her dissipated, and her form dissolved into the air, leaving nothing but a faint, lingering mist.

The storm began to subside, the wind dying down and the waves calming. The dark clouds that had covered the sky began to part, revealing the first rays of sunlight breaking through.

Elara and Seraphina stood together, their hands still glowing with the remnants of their magic. The air was filled with a sense of peace and relief, the oppressive darkness lifted.

The Aftermath

THE BATTLE HAD BEEN won, but at a great cost. The village of Marinia lay in ruins, the once vibrant community devastated by the storm and the battle. The villagers stood together, their faces filled with a mixture of relief and sorrow.

Elara surveyed the damage, her heart heavy with the weight of their losses. She had led them into battle, and they had fought bravely, but the cost had been high.

"We have won, but the price has been great," Elara said softly, her voice filled with sorrow. "We must rebuild and heal together."

Finn stepped forward, his eyes filled with pride and determination. "We will rebuild, Elara. We will stand together and create a brighter future."

The villagers nodded in agreement, their resolve unshaken. They began to work together, clearing the debris and rebuilding their homes. Elara and Seraphina used their magic to help, their combined strength and determination driving them forward.

A New Beginning

AS THE DAYS PASSED, the village of Marinia slowly began to heal. The villagers worked tirelessly to rebuild their homes and restore their community. The sea, once dark and turbulent under Morgana's influence, now shimmered with a serene beauty.

Elara felt a deep sense of peace and fulfillment. She had faced many challenges and overcome great obstacles, and she had formed deep connections with Seraphina and the villagers. She knew that there were still many mysteries to explore and many challenges to face, but she was ready for whatever lay ahead.

One evening, as the sun set over the ocean, Elara stood at the water's edge, gazing out at the horizon. The sea was calm and inviting, filled with the promise of new adventures and discoveries.

Seraphina emerged from the water, her eyes filled with gratitude and determination. "Thank you, Elara," she said softly. "You have set me free and restored balance to the sea. I am forever grateful."

Elara smiled, feeling a deep sense of fulfillment. "It has been an honor to help you, Seraphina. I look forward to our future adventures together."

Orin flew down to perch on Elara's shoulder, his golden eyes filled with wisdom and encouragement. "The journey has been long and challenging, but you have shown great courage and strength. I am proud to call you my friend."

Elara felt a deep sense of connection to her friends and to the magical world she had discovered. She knew that there were still many mysteries to explore and many challenges to face, but she was ready for whatever lay ahead.

And so, with the promise of new adventures and the support of her friends, Elara set off on a new journey, her heart filled with hope and her spirit unyielding. The echoes of her success resonated in her heart, a constant reminder of the bond she shared with Seraphina and the destiny that awaited them both.

The Legacy of the Battle

THE BATTLE AT SEA HAD left a lasting impact on the village of Marinia and its people. The villagers had faced their darkest fears and emerged stronger, their unity and determination a testament to their resilience.

Elara's bravery had inspired a new generation of heroes, young and old alike, who looked to her as a symbol of hope and courage. She became a mentor and guide, sharing her knowledge and experiences with those who sought to protect their home and their sea.

Seraphina continued to guard the sea, her presence a comforting and powerful force. She and Elara maintained a close bond, their friendship forged in the crucible of battle and strengthened by their shared experiences.

As the years passed, the story of Elara's journey and the battle at sea became legend, passed down through generations. The villagers honored her memory and the sacrifices made by all who had fought to protect their home.

The village of Marinia flourished, its people united by a common purpose and a deep connection to the sea. They worked together to preserve the balance and harmony that Elara and Seraphina had fought so hard to restore.

A New Era of Peace

WITH MORGANA'S DEFEAT and the restoration of balance to the sea, a new era of peace and prosperity began for the village of Marinia. The villagers celebrated their victories and honored their heroes, their hearts filled with gratitude and hope.

Elara continued to explore the mysteries of the sea, her adventures taking her to distant shores and uncharted waters. She encountered new challenges and formed new friendships, her journey a never-ending quest for knowledge and understanding.

Through it all, Elara remained a beacon of hope and courage, her legacy a reminder of the strength and resilience of the human spirit. She knew that there would always be challenges to face and mysteries to unravel, but she was ready for whatever lay ahead.

With Seraphina and Orin by her side, Elara set sail on a new adventure, her heart filled with hope and her spirit unyielding. The sea, with all its magic and mystery, awaited her, and she was ready to embrace her destiny.

The echoes of the past resonated in her heart, a constant reminder of the bond she shared with her friends and the legacy she had created. As the sun rose over the horizon, casting a golden glow over the ocean, Elara looked to the future with hope and determination, knowing that her journey was far from over.

Chapter 11: The Broken Curse

The Morning After the Battle

The sun rose gently over Marinia, casting a golden glow over the now peaceful village and its tranquil shores. The aftermath of the fierce battle with Morgana had left the villagers physically exhausted but spiritually invigorated. Elara, having led her people and allies to victory, felt a mixture of relief and sadness. The dark clouds that had once shrouded the sea were now dispersed, leaving a clear sky that promised new beginnings.

As Elara walked along the shore, she could still feel the lingering presence of magic in the air. The storm's memory was etched into the sands, but the peaceful waves gently lapping at the shore reassured her that they had succeeded in restoring balance. She had one more task to complete: ensuring that Seraphina's freedom from the curse was absolute and final.

The Ritual of Release

THE PREVIOUS NIGHT, after the victory against Morgana, Seraphina had told Elara of the final step required to break the curse completely. They needed to perform a Ritual of Release at sunrise. This ritual would involve the enchanted shell, the very object that had allowed Seraphina to communicate with the human world.

As the first rays of sunlight pierced the horizon, Elara gathered the villagers and led them to the cove where Seraphina waited, her ethereal form shimmering with a renewed vigor. Finn, Elara's father, carried the enchanted shell, its glow dimming as if it sensed the impending ritual.

The villagers formed a circle around the cove, their faces filled with hope and anticipation. Elara stepped forward, her heart heavy with the weight of the moment. She knew that freeing Seraphina might come at a great cost, but she was prepared to make any sacrifice for her friend.

Seraphina emerged from the water, her eyes reflecting the morning light. She smiled at Elara, her gratitude and determination evident.

"Are you ready, Seraphina?" Elara asked, her voice steady but tinged with emotion.

Seraphina nodded. "I am. This ritual will free me from the curse, but it may also sever my connection to the human world. Whatever happens, Elara, know that our friendship has meant everything to me."

Elara's heart ached at the thought of losing Seraphina, but she knew it was the right thing to do. "Let's begin," she said, her voice firm.

The Enchanted Shell Shatters

SERAPHINA AND ELARA stood at the center of the cove, the enchanted shell glowing softly between them. Seraphina began to chant the ancient incantations, her voice filled with a serene power. The villagers watched in awe as the air around them shimmered with magic.

As the incantations reached their peak, Elara felt a surge of energy course through her. She held the shell in her hands, its warmth radiating through her body. The shell began to vibrate, its glow intensifying.

Suddenly, a blinding light erupted from the shell, enveloping both Elara and Seraphina. The air crackled with energy, and Elara could feel the curse lifting, its dark tendrils unraveling and dissipating into the ether.

But as the light faded, the enchanted shell began to crack. A web of fractures spread across its surface, and with a final, shattering sound, the shell broke into countless pieces. The fragments fell into the water, disappearing beneath the waves.

Elara felt a pang of sorrow as she realized what the shattering of the shell meant. Seraphina was free from the curse, but the bond that had allowed her to communicate with the human world was severed.

Seraphina's form shimmered and began to fade. She looked at Elara, her eyes filled with both sadness and gratitude. "Thank you, Elara," she said softly. "You have given me my freedom. I will always cherish our friendship."

Elara's eyes filled with tears. "I will never forget you, Seraphina. Thank you for everything."

With a final, lingering glance, Seraphina vanished, her form dissolving into the water. The cove fell silent, and the villagers stood in a hushed reverence, understanding the magnitude of what had just occurred.

The Weight of Loss

THE DAYS FOLLOWING the ritual were filled with a profound sense of loss for Elara. She had gained so much on her journey, but losing Seraphina left an emptiness in her heart. She spent hours by the cove, reflecting on their adventures and the bond they had shared.

Finn noticed his daughter's sorrow and tried to comfort her. "Elara, you did something incredible. You freed Seraphina and saved our village. Your bravery and kindness will always be remembered."

Elara nodded, her eyes glistening with unshed tears. "I know, Father. But I miss her. She was more than a friend; she was a part of me."

Finn embraced Elara, offering her the solace of a father's love. "In time, you will find peace. Remember the good times you shared and let those memories guide you."

The villagers, too, rallied around Elara, offering their support and gratitude. They had all benefited from her courage and leadership, and they wanted to help her heal.

Honoring Seraphina

ELARA DECIDED TO HONOR Seraphina's memory by creating a memorial at the cove. She gathered the villagers and explained her plan. They all agreed, eager to contribute to the tribute for the mermaid who had played such a crucial role in their victory.

The memorial was a beautiful structure made of driftwood, seashells, and other treasures from the sea. At its center stood a statue of Seraphina, crafted by the village's most skilled artisans. The statue captured Seraphina's grace and strength, her eyes looking out to the horizon as if she were watching over them.

Elara placed a plaque at the base of the statue, inscribed with words of gratitude and remembrance. It read:

"In memory of Seraphina, the brave mermaid who taught us the true meaning of friendship and courage. May her spirit forever guide and protect us."

The villagers gathered around the memorial, sharing stories and memories of Seraphina. Elara felt a sense of closure and peace as she listened to their words. She knew that Seraphina's legacy would live on in their hearts.

Moving Forward

AS THE DAYS TURNED into weeks, Elara began to find a new sense of purpose. She threw herself into rebuilding the village and helping the villagers recover from the battle. Her leadership and determination inspired others, and together, they created a stronger, more united community.

Elara also continued her exploration of the sea, discovering new wonders and forging new alliances. She felt Seraphina's presence with her, guiding her on her adventures and reminding her of the bond they had shared.

One evening, as the sun set over the ocean, Elara stood at the shore, watching the waves. She felt a sense of calm and contentment, knowing that she had honored Seraphina's memory and found a way to move forward.

Orin flew down to perch on her shoulder, his golden eyes filled with wisdom and encouragement. "You have done well, Elara. Seraphina would be proud of you."

Elara smiled, feeling a deep connection to her friend. "Thank you, Orin. I couldn't have done it without you."

As they watched the sunset together, Elara felt a renewed sense of hope and determination. She knew that her journey was far from over, and that there were still many adventures to be had. But she also knew that she was not alone, and that the spirit of friendship and courage would always guide her.

The Legacy of Seraphina

THE MEMORIAL TO SERAPHINA became a place of pilgrimage for the villagers and travelers alike. People came from far and wide to pay their respects and draw inspiration from the story of Elara and Seraphina. The cove, once a place of battle and sorrow, was now a sanctuary of peace and reflection.

Elara often visited the memorial, leaving flowers and seashells as tokens of her love and gratitude. She felt a deep sense of connection to the place, knowing that it was a testament to the bond she and Seraphina had shared.

The village of Marinia flourished under Elara's leadership. The villagers worked together to rebuild and strengthen their community, their hearts united by the memory of their shared struggle and victory. They honored Elara as their hero, but she always reminded them that it was their collective strength and courage that had brought them through.

New Adventures

ELARA'S JOURNEY CONTINUED, filled with new challenges and discoveries. She explored distant shores, encountered mythical creatures, and forged alliances with other guardians of the sea. Her adventures were filled with wonder and excitement, but she always carried the memory of Seraphina with her.

One day, while exploring a hidden cave, Elara discovered an ancient artifact that radiated with powerful magic. She felt a familiar presence and realized that it was a gift from Seraphina, a reminder that their bond transcended time and space.

The artifact was a beautiful, intricately carved seashell, glowing with an ethereal light. Elara held it in her hands, feeling a surge of warmth and love. She knew that Seraphina was still with her, guiding her on her journey.

With the artifact in hand, Elara returned to Marinia, eager to share her discovery with the villagers. The artifact became a symbol of their connection to the sea and the enduring legacy of Seraphina.

A New Chapter

AS ELARA STOOD AT THE shore, watching the waves gently lap at the sand, she felt a sense of peace and fulfillment. She had faced many challenges, but she had also found strength and friendship in unexpected places. Her journey had been filled with both sorrow and joy, but she knew that it was far from over.

Elara looked out at the horizon, her heart filled with hope and determination. The sea, with all its magic and mystery, awaited her. She knew that there were still many adventures to be had and many mysteries to uncover.

With Seraphina's spirit guiding her and the support of her friends and community, Elara felt ready to face whatever lay ahead. The echoes of her past adventures resonated in her heart, a constant reminder of the bond she shared with Seraphina and the legacy they had created.

As the sun set over the ocean, casting a golden glow over the village of Marinia, Elara took a deep breath and set off on a new journey. The sea, with all its wonders and challenges, awaited her, and she was ready to embrace her destiny.

And so, with the promise of new adventures and the support of her friends, Elara began a new chapter in her life, her heart filled with hope and her spirit unyielding. The legacy of Seraphina lived on in her heart, a constant reminder of the power of friendship and the strength of the human spirit.

Chapter 12: The Return to Marinia

The Journey Back Home

The journey back to Marinia was long and arduous, but Elara's heart was light with the knowledge of her victory and the prospect of returning home. She had faced many challenges, from the depths of the ocean to the heights of the Mountain of Echoes, but she had emerged stronger and wiser. Now, with Seraphina's curse broken and the sea at peace, she felt a deep sense of fulfillment.

Elara and Orin traveled through forests and across rivers, their path illuminated by the soft glow of the enchanted artifact she had discovered in the hidden cave. The seashell, a gift from Seraphina, was a constant reminder of their bond and the journey they had shared.

As they neared Marinia, the landscape grew more familiar, the rolling hills and dense forests giving way to the open fields and rocky shores of her home. Elara felt a surge of anticipation and excitement. She had been away for so long, and she couldn't wait to see her family and friends again.

Arrival in Marinia

WHEN ELARA AND ORIN finally reached the outskirts of the village, they were greeted by the sight of familiar faces and the sound of joyous cheers. Word of her return had spread quickly, and the villagers had gathered to welcome her home.

Finn, Elara's father, was the first to embrace her. His eyes were filled with pride and relief. "Welcome home, Elara," he said, his voice choked with emotion. "You have done something incredible. We are all so proud of you."

Elara hugged her father tightly, feeling a rush of warmth and love. "Thank you, Father. It feels good to be home."

The villagers surrounded Elara, their faces beaming with admiration and gratitude. They had heard of her bravery and the challenges she had faced, and they were eager to hear her story.

"Tell us what happened, Elara," one of the villagers called out. "We want to know everything!"

Elara smiled, feeling a deep sense of connection to her community. "I will," she said. "But first, let's gather at the town square. I have much to share with you."

Sharing the Story of Seraphina

AS THE VILLAGERS MADE their way to the town square, Elara took a moment to collect her thoughts. She had experienced so much on her journey, and she wanted to convey the importance of what she had learned and the bond she had formed with Seraphina.

The town square was decorated with banners and flowers, a testament to the villagers' pride and joy. Elara stood at the center, her heart filled with a sense of purpose. She raised her hands, and the crowd fell silent, their eyes fixed on her.

"Thank you all for your warm welcome," Elara began, her voice steady and clear. "I have returned from a journey that took me to the farthest reaches of the sea and the highest peaks of the mountains. I have faced many challenges and learned valuable lessons. But most importantly, I have made a friend who has shown me the true meaning of courage and friendship."

Elara paused, her eyes scanning the crowd. She could see the anticipation and curiosity in their faces, and she felt a deep sense of responsibility to share her story with honesty and clarity.

"Her name is Seraphina," Elara continued. "She is a mermaid who was cursed by the sea witch Morgana. Seraphina and I formed a bond that transcended the boundaries of our worlds. Together, we fought to break the curse and restore balance to the sea."

The villagers listened intently as Elara recounted her journey. She spoke of the enchanted shell that had allowed her to communicate with Seraphina, the trials she had faced in the Whispering Woods and the Mountain of Echoes, and the final, dramatic battle against Morgana.

As she told her story, Elara felt a deep sense of connection to the sea and the magical world she had discovered. She wanted the villagers to understand the importance of protecting the sea and the creatures that lived within it.

The Importance of Protecting the Sea

"SERAPHINA TAUGHT ME many things," Elara said, her voice filled with emotion. "But one of the most important lessons she imparted was the need to protect the sea. The ocean is a vast and mysterious world, filled with beauty and wonder. But it is also fragile and vulnerable. We must take care of it, not just for ourselves, but for future generations."

The villagers nodded in agreement, their faces filled with understanding. They had always respected the sea, but Elara's words gave them a deeper appreciation for its importance and the need to protect it.

"We can start by taking simple actions," Elara continued. "We can reduce our waste, avoid harmful practices, and work together to preserve the natural beauty of our coastline. Every little effort counts, and together, we can make a difference."

Finn stepped forward, his eyes shining with pride. "Elara is right," he said. "We have always been a community that values our connection to the sea. Let us honor her journey and the lessons she has learned by committing ourselves to protect our beautiful ocean."

The villagers cheered, their hearts filled with a renewed sense of purpose. Elara felt a surge of gratitude and pride as she looked at the faces of her friends and family. They had always been there for her, and now, she knew they would stand together to protect the sea.

Honoring Seraphina's Memory

ELARA LED THE VILLAGERS to the memorial she had created for Seraphina at the cove. The beautiful structure, made of driftwood, seashells, and other treasures from the sea, stood as a testament to their friendship and the bravery they had shown.

The statue of Seraphina, crafted by the village's most skilled artisans, captured her grace and strength. The plaque at its base, inscribed with words of gratitude and remembrance, served as a constant reminder of the bond they had shared.

"In memory of Seraphina, the brave mermaid who taught us the true meaning of friendship and courage. May her spirit forever guide and protect us."

The villagers gathered around the memorial, sharing stories and memories of Seraphina. Elara felt a deep sense of peace as she listened to their words. She knew that Seraphina's legacy would live on in their hearts.

As the sun set over the ocean, casting a golden glow over the cove, Elara felt a sense of closure and fulfillment. She had honored Seraphina's memory and found a way to move forward. The sea, once a place of danger and darkness, was now a sanctuary of peace and reflection.

Rebuilding and Moving Forward

WITH THE BATTLE BEHIND them and the village united in their commitment to protect the sea, the villagers of Marinia set to work rebuilding their homes and strengthening their community. Elara threw herself into the effort, her leadership and determination inspiring others to work together.

The days were filled with hard work and camaraderie as the villagers cleared debris, repaired damaged buildings, and planted new gardens. Elara felt a deep sense of satisfaction as she watched the village come back to life. The scars of the battle were slowly healing, and a new sense of hope and optimism filled the air.

Elara also continued her exploration of the sea, discovering new wonders and forging new alliances. She felt Seraphina's presence with her, guiding her on her adventures and reminding her of the bond they had shared.

One day, while exploring a hidden reef, Elara discovered a vibrant underwater garden filled with colorful corals and exotic marine life. She felt a surge of joy as she swam through the garden, marveling at its beauty and diversity.

Elara knew that her journey was far from over. There were still many mysteries to explore and many challenges to face. But she felt a deep sense of confidence and determination, knowing that she had the strength and courage to overcome whatever lay ahead.

A New Era of Peace

AS THE VILLAGE OF MARINIA flourished, the villagers honored Elara as their hero and protector. Her bravery and determination had saved their home and restored balance to the sea. They celebrated her achievements and looked to her for guidance and inspiration.

Elara felt a deep sense of responsibility to her community and the sea. She knew that the bond she had formed with Seraphina was a gift, and she was determined to honor it by continuing to protect the ocean and its inhabitants.

The memorial to Seraphina became a place of pilgrimage for the villagers and travelers alike. People came from far and wide to pay their respects and draw inspiration from the story of Elara and Seraphina. The cove, once a place of battle and sorrow, was now a sanctuary of peace and reflection.

Elara often visited the memorial, leaving flowers and seashells as tokens of her love and gratitude. She felt a deep sense of connection to the place, knowing that it was a testament to the bond she and Seraphina had shared.

As the years passed, the story of Elara's journey and the battle at sea became legend, passed down through generations. The villagers honored her memory and the sacrifices made by all who had fought to protect their home.

A New Beginning

WITH THE SEA AT PEACE and the village flourishing, Elara felt a sense of fulfillment and contentment. She had faced many challenges and overcome great obstacles, but she had also found strength and friendship in unexpected places. Her journey had been filled with both sorrow and joy, but she knew that it was far from over.

Elara looked out at the horizon, her heart filled with hope and determination. The sea, with all its magic and mystery, awaited her. She knew that there were still many adventures to be had and many mysteries to uncover.

With Seraphina's spirit guiding her and the support of her friends and community, Elara felt ready to face whatever lay ahead. The echoes of her past adventures resonated in her heart, a constant reminder of the bond she shared with Seraphina and the legacy they had created.

As the sun set over the ocean, casting a golden glow over the village of Marinia, Elara took a deep breath and set off on a new journey. The sea, with all its wonders and challenges, awaited her, and she was ready to embrace her destiny.

And so, with the promise of new adventures and the support of her friends, Elara began a new chapter in her life, her heart filled with hope and her spirit unyielding. The legacy of Seraphina lived on in her heart, a constant reminder of the power of friendship and the strength of the human spirit.

Continuing the Legacy

ELARA'S COMMITMENT to protecting the sea and honoring Seraphina's memory extended beyond Marinia. She traveled to neighboring villages and coastal towns, sharing her story and encouraging others to take action to protect the ocean. Her message of unity and conservation resonated with many, and soon, a network of coastal communities was formed, dedicated to preserving the health and beauty of the sea.

These communities worked together to implement sustainable practices, reduce pollution, and protect marine life. They organized clean-up efforts, educational programs, and conservation initiatives, all inspired by Elara's leadership and the legacy of Seraphina.

Elara's travels took her to distant shores and exotic islands, where she discovered new species, explored hidden reefs, and forged alliances with other guardians of the sea. Her adventures were filled with wonder and excitement, but she always carried the memory of Seraphina with her.

One day, while exploring a remote island, Elara encountered a group of sea guardians who had heard of her journey and wanted to join her cause. They shared stories of their own struggles and triumphs, and together, they formed a powerful alliance dedicated to protecting the ocean and its inhabitants.

A Vision for the Future

AS ELARA CONTINUED her work, she began to envision a future where humans and the sea existed in harmony, each respecting and protecting the other. She knew that this vision would require dedication, cooperation, and a deep understanding of the interconnectedness of all life.

Elara and her allies worked tirelessly to promote this vision, organizing conferences, workshops, and collaborative projects. They reached out to scientists, educators, policymakers, and community leaders, building a diverse and powerful coalition dedicated to marine conservation.

Through their efforts, they achieved significant milestones, including the establishment of marine protected areas, the restoration of damaged ecosystems, and the implementation of sustainable fishing practices. These successes inspired others to join their cause, and the movement grew, spreading across continents and oceans.

Elara's vision for the future was not just about protecting the sea; it was about fostering a sense of connection and responsibility among all people. She believed that by understanding and respecting the natural world, humanity could achieve a more balanced and harmonious existence.

A Lasting Legacy

AS THE YEARS PASSED, Elara's work and the legacy of Seraphina continued to inspire and guide countless individuals and communities. The memorial at the cove remained a place of pilgrimage and reflection, a symbol of the enduring bond between humans and the sea.

Elara herself became a living legend, her story passed down through generations as a testament to the power of courage, friendship, and determination. She continued to explore, learn, and teach, always driven by her love for the sea and her commitment to its protection.

One evening, as Elara stood at the shore, watching the waves gently lap at the sand, she felt a deep sense of fulfillment and peace. She had faced many challenges and overcome great obstacles, but she had also found strength and friendship in unexpected places. Her journey had been filled with both sorrow and joy, but she knew that it was far from over.

With the sun setting over the ocean, casting a golden glow over the village of Marinia, Elara took a deep breath and set off on a new journey. The sea, with all its wonders and challenges, awaited her, and she was ready to embrace her destiny.

And so, with the promise of new adventures and the support of her friends, Elara began a new chapter in her life, her heart filled with hope and her spirit unyielding. The legacy of Seraphina lived on in her heart, a constant reminder of the power of friendship and the strength of the human spirit.

The echoes of her past adventures resonated in her heart, guiding her forward into a future filled with possibility and promise. Elara knew that as long as she remained true to her values and her vision, she could achieve anything.

The sea, with all its magic and mystery, awaited her, and Elara was ready to embrace the challenges and wonders that lay ahead. She knew that her journey was far from over, and she was excited to see where it would take her next.

With Seraphina's spirit guiding her and the support of her friends and community, Elara felt ready to face whatever lay ahead. The echoes of her past adventures resonated in her heart, a constant reminder of the bond she shared with Seraphina and the legacy they had created.

As the sun set over the horizon, Elara took a deep breath and set off on a new journey, her heart filled with hope and her spirit unyielding. The sea, with all its wonders and challenges, awaited her, and she was ready to embrace her destiny.

Chapter 13: The Mermaid's Gift

A Whisper in the Waves

The days of rebuilding and celebration in Marinia had brought a sense of peace and fulfillment to Elara, yet a longing lingered in her heart. Though Seraphina's physical presence was no longer with her, Elara often found herself standing by the shore, staring out at the endless expanse of the ocean, feeling the bond they shared resonate deeply within her.

One calm morning, as the first light of dawn kissed the horizon, Elara was drawn to the cove. The sea was a serene, glassy blue, and the gentle lapping of the waves seemed to whisper secrets just beyond her understanding. Standing at the water's edge, Elara closed her eyes and allowed the sounds of the sea to envelop her.

As she stood there, lost in the tranquility of the moment, a faint glow beneath the surface of the water caught her attention. Curious, Elara waded into the shallows, her fingers reaching out to grasp the source of the light. She felt something smooth and round, and as she pulled it from the water, she discovered a large, lustrous pearl, shimmering with an ethereal light.

The pearl pulsed gently in her hand, and Elara felt a surge of warmth and familiarity. It was as if a part of Seraphina's spirit had been captured within the pearl, a final gift from her friend to guide and protect her.

Holding the pearl close to her heart, Elara whispered, "Thank you, Seraphina."

The Power of the Pearl

ELARA BROUGHT THE PEARL back to the village, eager to uncover its secrets. She gathered the villagers in the town square, where they had so often met to discuss important matters. Finn, always by her side, stood with her as she explained the significance of the pearl.

"This pearl," Elara began, her voice filled with reverence, "was left to me by Seraphina. It is more than just a beautiful object; it holds the power to communicate with the sea and ensure the continued harmony between our village and the ocean."

The villagers murmured in awe and curiosity, their faces reflecting the same sense of wonder Elara felt. She knew that the pearl was a precious gift, not just for her, but for the entire community.

Elara decided to consult with the village's elder, Maelis, who had always been a source of wisdom and guidance. Together, they examined the pearl, seeking to understand its full potential.

Maelis held the pearl in her hands, her eyes closed in concentration. After a few moments, she smiled and handed the pearl back to Elara. "This is a powerful gift, Elara. The pearl holds the essence of Seraphina's magic, and it will allow you to communicate with the sea. You must use it wisely to protect and preserve the harmony between our village and the ocean."

Elara nodded, feeling a deep sense of responsibility. She vowed to honor Seraphina's memory by using the pearl to ensure the continued well-being of Marinia and the sea.

Communicating with the Sea

WITH THE PEARL IN HER possession, Elara began to explore its powers. She spent hours by the shore, holding the pearl and listening to the whispers of the waves. Slowly, she learned to understand the language of the sea, its rhythms and currents revealing secrets and stories that had been hidden from human ears.

One day, as she sat by the water's edge, Elara heard a faint, melodic voice emanating from the pearl. It was Seraphina's voice, gentle and soothing, guiding her in her efforts to communicate with the sea.

"Elara," the voice whispered, "the sea is a living, breathing entity, filled with wisdom and knowledge. Use the pearl to listen and learn, to protect and preserve. The sea will guide you, as I have guided you."

Elara felt a surge of gratitude and determination. With Seraphina's guidance, she knew she could use the pearl to strengthen the bond between Marinia and the ocean.

Ensuring Harmony

ELARA'S FIRST TASK was to use the pearl to address the environmental challenges that threatened the sea. She organized a series of community meetings, where she shared her newfound knowledge and encouraged the villagers to take action.

"We must work together to protect our beautiful ocean," Elara said. "The pearl has shown me the delicate balance that exists between the sea and our village. We must be mindful of our actions and take steps to preserve this harmony."

The villagers responded with enthusiasm and commitment. They organized clean-up efforts along the shoreline, removing debris and waste that had accumulated over time. They also implemented sustainable fishing practices, ensuring that the marine life thrived and the ecosystem remained healthy.

Elara used the pearl to monitor the health of the ocean, listening to the whispers of the waves and the currents. She could sense when the sea was in distress and took swift action to address any issues that arose. The villagers, inspired by her leadership, worked tirelessly to support her efforts.

As the months passed, the sea flourished. The waters around Marinia became clearer and more vibrant, teeming with marine life. The villagers felt a renewed sense of connection to the ocean, knowing that their efforts were making a difference.

A New Era of Collaboration

WITH THE PEARL'S GUIDANCE, Elara also fostered stronger ties with neighboring coastal communities. She traveled to distant shores, sharing her story and encouraging others to join the effort to protect the sea. Her message of unity and conservation resonated with many, and soon, a network of coastal communities was formed, dedicated to preserving the health and beauty of the ocean.

These communities worked together to implement sustainable practices, reduce pollution, and protect marine life. They organized conferences, workshops, and collaborative projects, building a diverse and powerful coalition dedicated to marine conservation.

Elara's vision for the future was not just about protecting the sea; it was about fostering a sense of connection and responsibility among all people. She believed that by understanding and respecting the natural world, humanity could achieve a more balanced and harmonious existence.

Through their efforts, they achieved significant milestones, including the establishment of marine protected areas, the restoration of damaged ecosystems, and the implementation of sustainable fishing practices. These successes inspired others to join their cause, and the movement grew, spreading across continents and oceans.

Honoring Seraphina's Memory

THE MEMORIAL TO SERAPHINA at the cove became a place of pilgrimage and reflection for the villagers and travelers alike. People came from far and wide to pay their respects and draw inspiration from the story of Elara and Seraphina. The cove, once a place of battle and sorrow, was now a sanctuary of peace and reflection.

Elara often visited the memorial, leaving flowers and seashells as tokens of her love and gratitude. She felt a deep sense of connection to the place, knowing that it was a testament to the bond she and Seraphina had shared.

One day, as Elara stood by the memorial, she felt the pearl in her hand begin to glow softly. She closed her eyes and listened to the whispers of the sea, feeling Seraphina's presence with her.

"Elara," Seraphina's voice echoed in her mind, "you have done so much to honor our bond and protect the sea. I am proud of you, my friend. Continue to use the pearl to guide and protect, and know that I am always with you."

Elara smiled, her heart filled with warmth and love. She knew that Seraphina's spirit would always be with her, guiding her on her journey.

A Legacy of Hope

AS THE YEARS PASSED, Elara's work and the legacy of Seraphina continued to inspire and guide countless individuals and communities. The network of coastal communities dedicated to marine conservation grew stronger, their efforts making a significant impact on the health and beauty of the ocean.

Elara became a living legend, her story passed down through generations as a testament to the power of courage, friendship, and determination. She continued to explore, learn, and teach, always driven by her love for the sea and her commitment to its protection.

One evening, as Elara stood at the shore, watching the waves gently lap at the sand, she felt a deep sense of fulfillment and peace. She had faced many challenges and overcome great obstacles, but she had also found strength and friendship in unexpected places. Her journey had been filled with both sorrow and joy, but she knew that it was far from over.

With the sun setting over the ocean, casting a golden glow over the village of Marinia, Elara took a deep breath and set off on a new journey. The sea, with all its wonders and challenges, awaited her, and she was ready to embrace her destiny.

And so, with the promise of new adventures and the support of her friends, Elara began a new chapter in her life, her heart filled with hope and her spirit unyielding. The legacy of Seraphina lived on in her heart, a constant reminder of the power of friendship and the strength of the human spirit.

Continuing the Legacy

ELARA'S COMMITMENT to protecting the sea and honoring Seraphina's memory extended beyond Marinia. She traveled to neighboring villages and coastal towns, sharing her story and encouraging others to take action to protect the ocean. Her message of unity and conservation resonated with many, and soon, a network of coastal communities was formed, dedicated to preserving the health and beauty of the sea.

These communities worked together to implement sustainable practices, reduce pollution, and protect marine life. They organized clean-up efforts, educational programs, and conservation initiatives, all inspired by Elara's leadership and the legacy of Seraphina.

Elara's travels took her to distant shores and exotic islands, where she discovered new species, explored hidden reefs, and forged alliances with other guardians of the sea. Her adventures were filled with wonder and excitement, but she always carried the memory of Seraphina with her.

One day, while exploring a remote island, Elara encountered a group of sea guardians who had heard of her journey and wanted to join her cause. They shared stories of their own struggles and triumphs, and together, they formed a powerful alliance dedicated to protecting the ocean and its inhabitants.

A Vision for the Future

AS ELARA CONTINUED her work, she began to envision a future where humans and the sea existed in harmony, each respecting and protecting the other. She knew that this vision would require dedication, cooperation, and a deep understanding of the interconnectedness of all life.

Elara and her allies worked tirelessly to promote this vision, organizing conferences, workshops, and collaborative projects. They reached out to scientists, educators, policymakers, and community leaders, building a diverse and powerful coalition dedicated to marine conservation.

Through their efforts, they achieved significant milestones, including the establishment of marine protected areas, the restoration of damaged ecosystems, and the implementation of sustainable fishing practices. These successes inspired others to join their cause, and the movement grew, spreading across continents and oceans.

Elara's vision for the future was not just about protecting the sea; it was about fostering a sense of connection and responsibility among all people. She believed that by understanding and respecting the natural world, humanity could achieve a more balanced and harmonious existence.

A Lasting Legacy

AS THE YEARS PASSED, Elara's work and the legacy of Seraphina continued to inspire and guide countless individuals and communities. The memorial at the cove remained a place of pilgrimage and reflection, a symbol of the enduring bond between humans and the sea.

Elara herself became a living legend, her story passed down through generations as a testament to the power of courage, friendship, and determination. She continued to explore, learn, and teach, always driven by her love for the sea and her commitment to its protection.

One evening, as Elara stood at the shore, watching the waves gently lap at the sand, she felt a deep sense of fulfillment and peace. She had faced many challenges and overcome great obstacles, but she had also found strength and friendship in unexpected places. Her journey had been filled with both sorrow and joy, but she knew that it was far from over.

With the sun setting over the ocean, casting a golden glow over the village of Marinia, Elara took a deep breath and set off on a new journey. The sea, with all its wonders and challenges, awaited her, and she was ready to embrace her destiny.

And so, with the promise of new adventures and the support of her friends, Elara began a new chapter in her life, her heart filled with hope and her spirit unyielding. The legacy of Seraphina lived on in her heart, a constant reminder of the power of friendship and the strength of the human spirit.

The echoes of her past adventures resonated in her heart, guiding her forward into a future filled with possibility and promise. Elara knew that as long as she remained true to her values and her vision, she could achieve anything.

The sea, with all its magic and mystery, awaited her, and Elara was ready to embrace the challenges and wonders that lay ahead. She knew that her journey was far from over, and she was excited to see where it would take her next.

With Seraphina's spirit guiding her and the support of her friends and community, Elara felt ready to face whatever lay ahead. The echoes of her past adventures resonated in her heart, a constant reminder of the bond she shared with Seraphina and the legacy they had created.

As the sun set over the horizon, Elara took a deep breath and set off on a new journey, her heart filled with hope and her spirit unyielding. The sea, with all its wonders and challenges, awaited her, and she was ready to embrace her destiny.

Chapter 14: The New Guardian

Embracing the Role

The dawn broke over Marinia, casting a warm golden light across the village and the shimmering sea. Elara stood at the water's edge, feeling the gentle lapping of the waves against her feet. She had returned from her travels, bringing with her a wealth of knowledge and a renewed sense of purpose. As she gazed out at the horizon, she knew that her journey had led her to this moment: she was ready to take on the role of the guardian of the shore.

With the enchanted pearl glowing softly in her hand, Elara felt a deep connection to the sea and the legacy of Seraphina. The mermaid's gift had given her the ability to communicate with the ocean, and she vowed to use this power to protect and preserve the delicate balance between the village and the sea.

The villagers had gathered to witness Elara's formal acceptance of her new role. They stood in a semicircle around her, their faces filled with admiration and trust. Finn, Elara's father, stepped forward, his eyes shining with pride.

"Elara, you have shown extraordinary courage and wisdom," Finn said, his voice strong and clear. "You have earned the right to be our guardian, and we are honored to stand with you."

Elara smiled, feeling the support of her community bolstering her resolve. "Thank you, Father. And thank you, everyone. I accept this responsibility with a full heart. Together, we will protect our shore and honor the legacy of Seraphina."

The villagers cheered, their voices ringing out in celebration. Elara felt a surge of pride and determination. She was ready to embrace her new role and the challenges that lay ahead.

Protecting the Shore

ELARA'S FIRST TASK as the guardian of the shore was to assess the current state of the coastline and identify any immediate threats. She spent hours walking along the beach, the enchanted pearl guiding her as she listened to the whispers of the waves. The sea spoke to her of erosion, pollution, and the delicate balance of marine life.

With this information, Elara called a meeting with the villagers to discuss the necessary actions to protect their shore. She stood before them, her voice filled with conviction.

"Our shore is beautiful, but it is also fragile," Elara began. "We must take steps to protect it from erosion, pollution, and overfishing. Together, we can create a sustainable future for our village and the sea."

The villagers listened intently, their faces reflecting their commitment to the cause. Elara outlined a series of initiatives, including planting native vegetation to prevent erosion, organizing regular beach clean-ups, and establishing fishing quotas to ensure the health of marine populations.

"We will need everyone's help," Elara said. "Each of us has a role to play in protecting our shore. Let's work together to make a difference."

The villagers responded with enthusiasm, eager to support Elara's efforts. They organized teams to plant vegetation along the dunes, removing invasive species and stabilizing the sandy soil. They set up a schedule for regular beach clean-ups, ensuring that the coastline remained free of debris and pollution.

Elara also worked closely with the village's fishermen to establish sustainable fishing practices. She used the enchanted pearl to communicate with the sea, learning about the breeding cycles and migration patterns of various fish species. With this knowledge, she helped the fishermen set quotas and seasons that would allow marine populations to thrive.

Educating the Community

IN ADDITION TO PROTECTING the shore, Elara knew that education was key to ensuring the long-term health of the ocean. She began organizing workshops and classes to teach the villagers about the mermaid's legacy and the magic of the sea.

Elara's first class was held in the village hall, where she had set up displays of marine life, shells, and artifacts from her travels. The villagers, young and old, gathered eagerly to learn from her.

"Welcome, everyone," Elara said, her voice warm and inviting. "Today, I want to share with you the story of Seraphina and the lessons she taught me. The sea is a wondrous place, filled with beauty and magic. But it is also fragile, and it needs our protection."

She began by recounting the tale of her journey with Seraphina, from their first meeting to the breaking of the curse. The villagers listened in rapt attention, their eyes wide with wonder.

"Seraphina's legacy is one of courage, friendship, and respect for the natural world," Elara continued. "She showed me that we are all connected, and that our actions have a profound impact on the world around us."

Elara then moved on to practical lessons about marine conservation. She explained the importance of protecting coral reefs, maintaining clean beaches, and preserving marine habitats. She demonstrated how to identify different species of fish and shellfish, and how to use sustainable practices to ensure their survival.

The villagers were enthusiastic learners, asking questions and sharing their own experiences. Elara encouraged them to take what they had learned and apply it in their daily lives.

"Each of us has the power to make a difference," Elara said. "Whether it's picking up litter on the beach, supporting sustainable fishing, or teaching our children about the magic of the sea, we can all contribute to a healthier, more vibrant ocean."

Building Alliances

AS THE GUARDIAN OF the shore, Elara knew that protecting the sea required collaboration and support from beyond Marinia. She reached out to neighboring coastal communities, sharing her story and inviting them to join her efforts.

Elara traveled to distant villages and towns, using the enchanted pearl to communicate with the sea and learn about the unique challenges each community faced. She met with local leaders, fishermen, and conservationists, forging alliances and building a network of support.

In each community, Elara shared the lessons she had learned from Seraphina and the importance of marine conservation. She organized workshops, clean-up efforts, and collaborative projects, fostering a sense of unity and shared responsibility.

One of Elara's most significant achievements was the establishment of a regional marine protected area. Working with leaders from several coastal communities, she helped to create a network of protected zones where marine life could thrive without the threat of overfishing or pollution.

The marine protected area became a model for conservation, attracting attention and support from scientists, policymakers, and environmental organizations. Elara's efforts were recognized and celebrated, and she was invited to speak at conferences and events, sharing her vision for a sustainable future.

The Magic of the Sea

THROUGHOUT HER WORK, Elara never lost sight of the magic and wonder of the sea. She continued to explore the ocean, discovering new species, hidden reefs, and underwater caves. The enchanted pearl guided her, its glow a constant reminder of Seraphina's presence.

One day, while diving in a remote part of the ocean, Elara discovered a breathtaking underwater garden. The coral formations were vibrant and colorful, teeming with marine life. Schools of fish swam in intricate patterns, and delicate sea anemones swayed gently in the currents.

Elara felt a profound sense of awe and gratitude as she swam through the garden. She knew that this was a place of magic, a testament to the beauty and resilience of the natural world.

Using the enchanted pearl, Elara communicated with the sea, learning about the delicate balance that maintained this underwater paradise. She felt a deep connection to the ocean, understanding that her role as guardian was both a privilege and a responsibility.

Elara returned to Marinia with stories and images of the underwater garden, eager to share the magic with the villagers. She organized a special event at the cove, where she projected underwater footage and shared her experiences.

The villagers were mesmerized by the beauty of the underwater world. Children's eyes widened in wonder as they watched the vibrant corals and graceful marine life. Adults listened intently as Elara explained the importance of protecting these fragile ecosystems.

"The sea is filled with wonders beyond our imagination," Elara said, her voice filled with passion. "It is our duty to protect these magical places and ensure that future generations can experience their beauty. Together, we can make a difference."

Facing New Threats

AS THE GUARDIAN OF the shore, Elara was vigilant in protecting the coast from threats. She knew that the ocean faced many challenges, from climate change to pollution to illegal fishing. She worked tirelessly to address these issues, using the enchanted pearl to guide her efforts.

One day, Elara received a distressing message from the sea. The currents whispered of a large vessel dumping toxic waste into the ocean, causing harm to marine life and polluting the waters. Elara knew she had to act quickly.

She organized a team of villagers and allies from neighboring communities to investigate the situation. They set out in boats, following the directions provided by the enchanted pearl. As they approached the area, they saw the damage firsthand: dead fish floating on the surface, discolored water, and the faint smell of chemicals in the air.

Elara felt a surge of anger and determination. She knew that they had to stop the vessel and hold those responsible accountable. She used the enchanted pearl to call upon the sea, asking for its help.

The ocean responded, sending powerful waves to rock the offending vessel. The crew, startled by the sudden turbulence, ceased their dumping and scrambled to stabilize the ship. Elara and her team approached, demanding that the crew stop their illegal activities and clean up the mess they had made.

With the threat of further action from the sea, the crew complied. They began to collect the toxic waste and promised to never return. Elara and her team monitored the cleanup efforts, ensuring that the waters were restored to their natural state.

The incident served as a powerful reminder of the challenges they faced and the importance of vigilance. Elara knew that her role as guardian was ongoing, and she remained committed to protecting the shore and the sea from harm.

A Legacy of Hope

AS THE YEARS PASSED, Elara's efforts to protect the shore and educate the community bore fruit. The village of Marinia flourished, its coastline vibrant and healthy. The villagers felt a deep connection to the sea, understanding the importance of their actions and the impact they had on the natural world.

Elara's work extended beyond Marinia, as coastal communities around the region adopted her vision for marine conservation. Together, they created a network of protected areas, sustainable practices, and educational programs that ensured the health and beauty of the ocean for generations to come.

Elara herself became a symbol of hope and resilience, her story inspiring countless individuals to take action and protect the natural world. She continued to explore, learn, and teach, always guided by the magic of the sea and the legacy of Seraphina.

One evening, as Elara stood at the shore, watching the sun set over the ocean, she felt a deep sense of fulfillment and peace. She knew that her journey had been filled with challenges, but it had also been a journey of growth, discovery, and connection.

With the enchanted pearl glowing softly in her hand, Elara felt Seraphina's presence with her. She knew that their bond was eternal, and that the lessons she had learned would guide her always.

As the stars began to twinkle in the night sky, Elara took a deep breath and set off on a new journey. The sea, with all its wonders and challenges, awaited her, and she was ready to embrace her destiny.

A New Generation of Guardians

ELARA UNDERSTOOD THAT the legacy of protecting the sea must be passed on to future generations. She began to mentor young villagers, sharing her knowledge and experiences with them. She taught them about the magic of the sea, the importance of conservation, and the responsibilities of being a guardian.

Among her students was a young girl named Lyra, who showed a remarkable affinity for the ocean. Lyra was curious and eager to learn, always asking questions and seeking to understand the mysteries of the sea. Elara saw great potential in her and took her under her wing.

Together, Elara and Lyra explored the coastline, diving into the depths of the ocean and discovering hidden wonders. Elara taught Lyra how to use the enchanted pearl to communicate with the sea and understand its rhythms and currents.

Lyra quickly became proficient, her bond with the ocean growing stronger each day. She learned to listen to the whispers of the waves and use her knowledge to protect and preserve the marine environment.

Elara felt a deep sense of pride and fulfillment as she watched Lyra grow into a capable and dedicated guardian. She knew that the future of the shore was in good hands.

The Next Chapter

AS LYRA TOOK ON MORE responsibilities, Elara felt a sense of peace and satisfaction. She knew that her work as a guardian had made a difference, and she was confident that the legacy of protecting the sea would continue.

One evening, as Elara and Lyra stood together on the shore, watching the sun set over the ocean, Elara felt a deep sense of connection and gratitude. She handed the enchanted pearl to Lyra, her eyes filled with pride.

"Lyra, you have shown great courage and wisdom," Elara said. "You are ready to take on the role of guardian. This pearl is a gift from Seraphina, and it will guide you as it has guided me."

Lyra accepted the pearl, her eyes shining with determination. "Thank you, Elara. I will honor Seraphina's legacy and continue to protect the sea."

Elara smiled, feeling a sense of fulfillment and peace. She knew that her journey had come full circle, and that the future of the shore was in good hands.

With the promise of new adventures and the support of her friends, Elara began a new chapter in her life, her heart filled with hope and her spirit unyielding. The legacy of Seraphina lived on in her heart, a constant reminder of the power of friendship and the strength of the human spirit.

As the stars twinkled in the night sky, Elara and Lyra stood together, watching the waves gently lap at the shore. The sea, with all its wonders and challenges, awaited them, and they were ready to embrace their destiny.

And so, with the promise of new adventures and the support of their community, Elara and Lyra embarked on a new journey, their hearts filled with hope and their spirits unyielding. The legacy of Seraphina lived on in their hearts, a constant reminder of the power of friendship and the strength of the human spirit. The sea, with all its magic and mystery, awaited them, and they were ready to embrace the challenges and wonders that lay ahead.

Chapter 15: The Whisper of the Future

The Legend of Elara

Years passed, and the story of Elara, the girl who befriended a mermaid and became the guardian of the shore, grew into a legend. Her name became synonymous with courage, wisdom, and a deep love for the sea. The villagers of Marinia and the surrounding coastal communities kept her memory alive, passing down her story from one generation to the next.

Children gathered around their grandparents, wide-eyed and eager, as they listened to tales of Elara's adventures. They heard about her journey with Seraphina, the battle against Morgana, and her tireless efforts to protect the ocean. The enchanted pearl, the magical shell, and the underwater garden became part of the fabric of their imaginations.

Elara herself had become a symbol of hope and resilience. Though she had long since passed the role of guardian to Lyra and other dedicated protectors, her spirit continued to inspire those who heard her story. Her legacy was evident in the thriving coastal communities, the pristine beaches, and the healthy marine ecosystems that stretched along the shoreline.

A New Generation

AS TIME WENT ON, A new generation of children grew up hearing about Elara and Seraphina. Among them was a curious and adventurous boy named Finnian, named after Elara's father. Finnian was captivated by the stories of Elara's bravery and the magical world of the sea. He often wandered along the beach, dreaming of his own adventures and longing to discover the secrets of the ocean.

One sunny afternoon, Finnian was exploring a hidden cove near his village. The cove was a place of tranquility and beauty, with crystal-clear water and colorful coral formations. As he waded through the shallows, he noticed a faint glow beneath the surface. His heart raced with excitement as he reached down and felt something smooth and round in his hand.

Finnian pulled the object from the water and gasped in amazement. It was an enchanted shell, similar to the one described in the legends of Elara and Seraphina. The shell glowed softly, its surface adorned with intricate patterns and symbols. Finnian knew that he had discovered something extraordinary.

The Discovery

FINNIAN HELD THE ENCHANTED shell close to his heart, feeling a sense of connection and wonder. He hurried back to the village, eager to share his discovery with his friends and family. The villagers gathered around him, their eyes wide with astonishment as they beheld the glowing shell.

"This is the enchanted shell from the legends!" Finnian exclaimed. "It must have been left behind by Elara or Seraphina. It's a sign that their magic is still with us."

The villagers murmured in excitement, their faces filled with awe and curiosity. Lyra, now an elder and the guardian of the shore, stepped forward to examine the shell. Her eyes shone with recognition and reverence.

"This shell is indeed enchanted," Lyra said, her voice filled with emotion. "It holds the magic of Seraphina and the legacy of Elara. Finnian, you have discovered a great treasure. We must honor it and learn from it."

Finnian felt a surge of pride and responsibility. He knew that the shell was a link to the past and a key to the future. He was determined to uncover its secrets and continue the legacy of Elara and Seraphina.

The Whisper of the Shell

THAT EVENING, THE VILLAGERS gathered around a bonfire on the beach. The enchanted shell was placed in the center, its soft glow illuminating their faces. Finnian sat next to Lyra, his heart pounding with anticipation as she began to speak.

"The enchanted shell holds the whispers of the sea," Lyra explained. "It can communicate with the ocean and reveal its secrets. We must listen carefully and learn from its wisdom."

She placed her hands on the shell and closed her eyes, her face serene and focused. The villagers watched in hushed silence as the shell began to emit a faint, melodic hum. Finnian leaned forward, straining to hear the whispers that emanated from within.

The hum grew louder, and the air around them seemed to shimmer with magic. Finnian felt a tingling sensation in his hands and feet, as if the energy of the shell was flowing through him. He closed his eyes and let the sound wash over him, listening intently to the whispers of the sea.

The voice of Seraphina echoed in his mind, gentle and soothing. "Finnian, you have discovered the enchanted shell and the legacy of Elara. The sea has chosen you to continue their work. Use the shell to communicate with the ocean, protect its creatures, and preserve its beauty."

Finnian's heart swelled with pride and determination. He opened his eyes and saw the faces of his friends and family, their expressions filled with trust and hope. He knew that he had a great responsibility, but he also knew that he was not alone.

Continuing the Legacy

OVER THE NEXT FEW WEEKS, Finnian dedicated himself to learning from the enchanted shell and the wisdom of the sea. He spent hours by the water's edge, listening to the whispers and gaining insights into the delicate balance of marine life. Lyra mentored him, sharing her knowledge and experiences, and helping him understand the importance of his role.

Finnian also began to teach the other children in the village about the magic of the sea and the legacy of Elara and Seraphina. He organized workshops and excursions, taking them to the hidden cove and other special places along the coastline. Together, they explored the underwater world, discovering the beauty and wonder that lay beneath the surface.

The children were eager learners, their eyes wide with excitement and curiosity. They listened to Finnian's stories and followed his guidance, understanding that they, too, had a role to play in protecting the ocean.

One day, while exploring a tide pool with a group of children, Finnian discovered a rare and beautiful sea creature. It was a small, iridescent seahorse, its delicate fins shimmering in the sunlight. The children gathered around, their faces filled with awe.

"This seahorse is a symbol of the magic and beauty of the sea," Finnian said. "We must protect it and its habitat. Remember, every action we take can make a difference."

The children nodded, their faces filled with determination. They carefully observed the seahorse, learning about its behavior and habitat. Finnian felt a deep sense of pride and fulfillment, knowing that the legacy of Elara and Seraphina was alive and well in the next generation.

Challenges and Triumphs

AS FINNIAN GREW OLDER, he faced many challenges in his role as a guardian. Climate change, pollution, and overfishing continued to threaten the health of the ocean. Finnian knew that he had to be vigilant and proactive in addressing these issues.

He worked closely with Lyra and other coastal communities, organizing campaigns to raise awareness and promote sustainable practices. They lobbied for stronger environmental protections and implemented innovative solutions to reduce pollution and preserve marine habitats.

One of Finnian's greatest achievements was the creation of an ocean sanctuary, a vast protected area where marine life could thrive without the threat of human interference. The sanctuary became a haven for endangered species and a model for conservation efforts around the world.

The enchanted shell continued to guide Finnian, its whispers providing insights and inspiration. He felt a deep connection to the sea, understanding that his role as a guardian was both a privilege and a responsibility.

One evening, as Finnian stood on the beach, watching the sunset, he heard a familiar voice in his mind. It was Seraphina, her tone filled with pride and affection.

"Finnian, you have done well," she said. "You have honored the legacy of Elara and protected the sea. The future is bright, and the magic of the ocean is in good hands."

Finnian smiled, feeling a sense of fulfillment and peace. He knew that his journey was far from over, but he also knew that he had the strength and wisdom to face whatever challenges lay ahead.

A New Beginning

AS THE YEARS PASSED, Finnian continued to serve as a guardian, protecting the shore and educating the community about the importance of marine conservation. He mentored a new generation of children, passing on the knowledge and values he had learned from Lyra and the enchanted shell.

One day, while exploring the hidden cove with a group of children, Finnian noticed a faint glow beneath the surface of the water. His heart raced with excitement as he reached down and felt something smooth and round in his hand.

He pulled the object from the water and gasped in amazement. It was another enchanted shell, glowing softly with an ethereal light. The children gathered around, their faces filled with wonder.

"This is a sign," Finnian said, his voice filled with reverence. "The magic of the sea is alive and well. We must continue to protect it and honor the legacy of Elara and Seraphina."

The children nodded, their eyes shining with determination. They knew that they had a great responsibility, but they also knew that they were not alone.

As Finnian held the enchanted shell, he felt a deep sense of connection and wonder. He knew that the story of Elara and Seraphina would continue, and that the magic of the sea would be passed on to future generations.

The Whisper of the Future

AS THE SUN SET OVER the ocean, casting a golden glow over the village of Marinia, Finnian stood on the beach, holding the enchanted shell. The waves lapped gently at the shore, their whispers filled with the promise of new adventures and discoveries.

Finnian closed his eyes and listened to the whispers of the sea. He felt a sense of peace and fulfillment, knowing that he was part of something greater than himself. The legacy of Elara and Seraphina lived on in his heart, a constant reminder of the power of friendship and the strength of the human spirit.

As the stars twinkled in the night sky, Finnian opened his eyes and looked out at the horizon. The sea, with all its wonders and challenges, awaited him, and he was ready to embrace his destiny.

And so, with the promise of new adventures and the support of his friends and community, Finnian began a new chapter in his life, his heart filled with hope and his spirit unyielding. The legacy of Elara and Seraphina lived on, a constant reminder of the magic of the sea and the importance of protecting it for future generations.

The whispers of the sea echoed in Finnian's mind, guiding him forward into a future filled with possibility and promise. He knew that as long as he remained true to his values and his vision, he could achieve anything.

The sea, with all its magic and mystery, awaited him, and Finnian was ready to embrace the challenges and wonders that lay ahead. He knew that his journey was far from over, and he was excited to see where it would take him next.

With the enchanted shell in his hand and the support of his friends and community, Finnian felt ready to face whatever lay ahead. The echoes of his past adventures resonated in his heart, a constant reminder of the bond he shared with Elara and Seraphina and the legacy they had created.

As the sun rose over the horizon, casting a golden glow over the village of Marinia, Finnian took a deep breath and set off on a new journey. The sea, with all its wonders and challenges, awaited him, and he was ready to embrace his destiny.

Don't miss out!

Visit the website below and you can sign up to receive emails whenever Patrick William Lee publishes a new book. There's no charge and no obligation.

https://books2read.com/r/B-A-FLRYB-RHSZD

BOOKS 2 READ

Connecting independent readers to independent writers.

Did you love *The Mermaid's Whisper*? Then you should read *Tales of the Whispering Forest*[1] by Patrick William Lee!

In "Tales of the Whispering Forest," join Elara and Finn on an epic adventure through a mystical forest filled with ancient secrets and magical beings. From discovering the enchanted grove to uncovering the legend of the Whispering Trees, they face cunning tricksters, powerful witches, and dark forces. Guided by a prophecy, they embark on a quest for the legendary Silver Leaf, unlocking the ability to communicate with the forest and confronting ultimate challenges that test their bravery, wisdom, and unity. Their journey will determine the fate of the forest and transform them into heroes.

---

1. https://books2read.com/u/4Xlqna

2. https://books2read.com/u/4Xlqna

About the Author

Patrick William Lee is a renowned author celebrated for his enchanting tales of magic and wonder. Specializing in the genres of fairy tales, folk tales, legends, and mythology, Patrick weaves stories that transport readers to fantastical realms where the impossible becomes reality. With a deep love for folklore and a talent for crafting timeless narratives, his books captivate the imaginations of readers young and old. When he's not writing, Patrick enjoys exploring ancient forests, studying mythical creatures, and sharing his passion for storytelling with audiences around the world. His works continue to inspire and delight, leaving a lasting impact on the world of literature.